S. Baring-Gould

One hundred sermon sketches for extempore preachers

S. Baring-Gould

One hundred sermon sketches for extempore preachers

ISBN/EAN: 9783741194153

Manufactured in Europe, USA, Canada, Australia, Japa

Cover: Foto ©Andreas Hilbeck / pixelio.de

Manufactured and distributed by brebook publishing software
(www.brebook.com)

S. Baring-Gould

One hundred sermon sketches for extempore preachers

ONE HUNDRED

SERMON SKETCHES

FOR

EXTEMPORE PREACHERS.

BY THE

REV. S. BARING-GOULD, M.A.,

AUTHOR OF
"ORIGIN AND DEVELOPMENT OF RELIGIOUS BELIEF,"
"CURIOUS MYTHS OF THE MIDDLE AGES," "POST-MEDIÆVAL PREACHERS," ETC.

FOURTH EDITION.

LONDON:
JOSEPH MASTERS AND CO., 78, NEW BOND STREET.
MDCCCLXXVII.

LONDON:
PRINTED BY JOSEPH MASTERS AND CO.,
ALBION BUILDINGS, BARTHOLOMEW CLOSE, E.C.

PREFACE.

THESE Sermon Sketches are published in the hopes that they may be of some assistance to missionary preachers among the poor in large towns, or among agricultural labourers in the country.

Living, as the writer does, in the country, with very little parochial work on his hands, he has been often asked by hard-worked priests, who have not time to collect material, and yet have to preach very frequently, to produce for their use a book of sketches for mission sermons.

This work is the answer to this request. The sketches are not intended for use among educated people, nor are they at all suitable for written sermons. They have been noted down for a guide to the author when preaching extempore, and he has here filled them out a little fuller for the assistance of others.

The doctrine in some may be more advanced than all who use the book may be prepared to endorse. But the author has not thought well to dilute it; for the time has come when Catholic clergy must speak out boldly, and the trumpet of doctrine must give no uncertain sound, but ring shrill and clear for the battle.

Feast of S. Vincent of Paul, 1871.

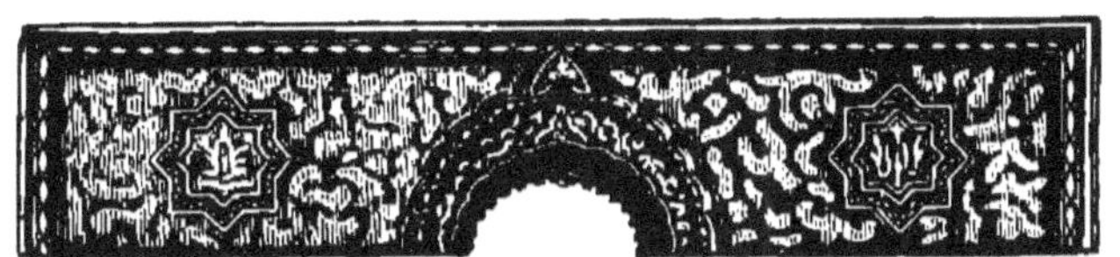

CONTENTS.

SERMON SKETCHES.

I.

THE BRIEFNESS OF THE PLEASURE OF SIN.

"But Jonathan . . . . put forth the end of the rod that was in his hand, and dipped it in an honeycomb, and put his hand to his mouth."— 1 Sam. xiv. 27.

Introduction. Narrate how Jonathan went over and captured the garrison of the Philistines, along with his armour-bearer. How, after a panic had fallen upon the enemy, the Philistines fled. How Saul pursued, and how he took an oath that any one who ate till the victory was complete, should be put to death. How Jonathan, not having heard the oath, did as is written in the text. He received sentence of death, but was finally spared at the intercession of the people.

Application. Now we also are engaged in a great battle with the Philistines,—the Devil, and all his host. We have to pursue him, for the victory is ours, we must not halt in the fight, to enjoy the pleasures of sin for a season, lest the sentence of death fall on us.

Point I. *The pleasure of sin is like that honey in the wilderness.*

How oft do you not say, in the midst of the battle of life: Oh! how sweet in this world is the honey of sinful pleasure dropping from the trees on all sides of us! May we not put forth the end of the rod and taste of it!

Oh! that dazzling pleasure of sense which made you halt in your onward career, which turned you from the pursuit, which distracted you from the work you had to do, which made you forget your mission!

Did you not taste thereof? Did you not say, Let me put forth the end of the rod and dip it, and taste? Mark you, only a drop from the end of the rod, and then you put out your hand and took the whole comb, and crushed it into your mouth!

Oh! that piece of vanity, that scheme of this world, touched at first and then becoming all-absorbing, all-occupying, to the forgetfulness of everything else!

Oh! that habit of indulgence of intemperate appetite yielded to slightly, then more, and then given way to entirely!

Oh! that spirit of envy growing stronger and stronger, the opportunity to resent a wrong given way to, because revenge is honey-sweet, till the whole heart is poisoned with rancour!

Oh! the sweet first taste! the luscious honey drop! the lightening of the eyes by the pleasure for one moment!—and then—

Point II. *This know, that thou shalt surely die!*

Yes! that is the sentence against sin. It is the sentence which was pronounced in Eden against the first sin:—"But of the tree of the knowledge of good and evil, thou shalt not eat of it: for in the day that thou eatest thereof thou shalt surely die." It is of this that the Apostle speaks when he says, "The wages of sin is death."

And now weigh that drop of honey against this pain of death. How its sweetness disappears in the balance.

Imagine one hereafter looking back on the indulgence of the past, and remembering what he has lost, what he has incurred, by yielding to the desire of putting forth the end of the rod that was in his hand, and tasting of the honey.

Think of the bitterness of spirit, the anguish of remorse, the weight of that sentence of eternal death, and all for that forbidden pleasure, that honey that dripped from the tree, as he passed on his way through life.

Conclusion. But is there no hope of escape, no chance of life, for one who has tasted, and so broken the commandment? The people pleaded with the king, and reminded him that Jonathan was his son, and the king pardoned Jonathan. Yes, thanks be to GOD! there is hope for us yet. The people of GOD, His Church, is ever interceding for the sinner; from every corner of the earth the great wave of intercessory prayer rolls, which breaks before the throne of GOD, a mighty wave of prayer that GOD will pardon the sinner, and remit the sentence of death, for the sake of His Only Begotten SON, JESUS CHRIST.

By the strength of that great prayer of intercession, and by the merits of CHRIST JESUS, there is hope of escape, and chance of life for the sinner.

II.

THE MEASURE OF SIN.

"*An ephah goeth forth.*"—Zech. v. 6.

Introduction. This vision of Zechariah signifies the iniquity of the Jewish people, gradually increasing till it was filled up by their rejection of CHRIST and of the HOLY GHOST. In the vision, the prophet saw a measure, called an ephah; the great Wickedness was cast into it, and then the ephah was closed with lead. "He said, This is wickedness. And he cast it into the midst of the ephah; and he cast the weight of lead upon the mouth thereof." Observe, this is the measure of the iniquity of the people of Israel; when it is filled, it is closed with lead. But that was not all, the ephah was carried away from its place; "They lifted up the ephah between the earth and heaven. Then said I to the angel that talked with me, Whither do these bear the ephah? And he said unto me, To build a house in the land of Shinar." This has reference to the Mystery of Iniquity and the reign of Antichrist, to which I will not now further allude.

Subject. But what I want you to observe is this. When the measure of iniquity was full, two results followed. It was covered with lead, and it was carried away out of its place.

And has not this been fulfilled with the Jewish nation? When the crowning iniquity of rejection, first of the testimony of the FATHER, speaking through Moses and the Prophets, and then of the testimony of CHRIST Himself coming in person, and lastly of the testimony of the HOLY GHOST, had filled the measure, then there descended upon them the lead of Impenitence and Unbelief, and they were carried away out of their own land.

Point I. *To every man there is a fixed measure of sin.*

For nations we know this exists; you may remember that the promise was made to Abraham, that in the fourth generation the land would be given him. Why not till the fourth generation? Because, we are told, not till then would be fulfilled the measure of the iniquities of the Amorites.

And so it is with individuals.

Oh! my brethren, how cautious we should be, how fearful of adding sin to sin. The next sin may be but a very little one, but it may be the last, *the one* wanted to fill up the measure.

You have given way to drunkenness, to evil speaking, to impurity, to lying—one more act, what will it matter? One glass more! what is there in one glass? One bitter slander more! what is there in one speech? One foul act more, only one! what matters another, just another, when there have been so many?

But what if that one glass, that one word, that one foul act fill the measure? And then down comes the lead and away you are borne!

Yes, there is a fixed measure before each, *varying* according to circumstances; to one a measure larger than to another, according as have been his opportunities, but to each *just*.

Point II. *The result of the filling of the measure is Final Impenitence or Death.*

Final Impenitence is typified by the lead; Death is symbolised by the carrying away to Shinar.

When the measure is full, when every opportunity of repentance has been rejected, when amendment has never been sought, when conscience has been persistently stifled, when sin has become habitual, till the measure is full, then what do we find?

We find that the faculty of Repentance is withdrawn, that Conscience ceases to speak, and that the desire for something better is completely and irrevocably lost. The power and the desire to rise and shake off evil habits, are gone—even the sense that there is anything better, nobler, truer in a different life, has disappeared.

Or else, we find that death comes and carries away him whose measure of iniquity is filled up; not always a sudden death, but sometimes it is so, and sometimes also that death is self-sought by him who finds that everything earth can give disgusts, but yet who has no aspirations for anything that is heavenly.

Conclusion. And now, what is the practical lesson to be carried home? It is this: Great scrupulousness about continuing in sin. When sin has been added to sin, by true repentance and sacramental confession empty the measure, fearing lest, by too long delay, it brim over, and the lead of Impenitence descend, or Death come and carry you away.

III.

THE NECESSITY OF PRECAUTION.

"*He crept under the elephant, and thrust him under and slew him; whereupon the elephant fell down upon him, and there he died.*"—1 Maccab. vi. 46.

Introduction. An account of the circumstances.

Application. Many a sinner is victorious through the grace of God, and in some great struggle with temptation, or an evil life, comes forth victorious. Some great battle, some season of mighty wrestling, of strife with the powers of evil; a conversion of the soul from sin. Then too many suppose all is over, the work is accomplished, there is nothing further to be feared.

Nevertheless a great danger remains. The elephant may be thrust through and slain, but the carcase remains to fall and crush.

Point I. *The Habit of Sin remains.*

At first, when a man has repented and confessed his sin, and has turned to GOD, all seems fair; he has no struggle for a moment or two, heaven is bright above him, the path of virtue smiles before him. But soon the dead elephant falls. The habit makes itself felt; he is under constraint, for he has to break away from, not merely sin itself, which he has slain, but the habit which has become a second nature, and that is a dead weight bearing him down. Well for him if it do not crush him, and slay his new-born spiritual life.

We hear it said that every man has got a skeleton in his closet. I do not know what truth there may be in that statement. But I do know, that every man who is striving to lead a better life than of old, is oppressed with a dead elephant.

Instance the habit of drinking, or habit of swearing.

Illustration. Have you never dreamt that you wanted to go a certain road, but that countless threads attached to your legs and arms held you back, and that advance you could not? Such are habits, the little threads constraining you from going in the newly chosen road, and dragging you back into that you were wont to walk in.

Precaution I. Against this dead weight of Habit, constant watchfulness and self-examination will alone prevail.

Point II. *Spiritual Pride.*

This is a most serious peril to the soul newly converted, and tasting that the Lord is gracious.

S. Bernard gave this good advice: "Fear when you receive favours from God; fear more when you lose them; fear most when you recover them." Fear when God has given you anything. In your Baptism, in your Confirmation, you received precious gifts—fear is the best guardian of those treasures. If you have lost them, fear—fear to be out of favour with God, to have incurred His wrath, to be estranged from Him! But fear most when you have recovered your place, by sincere repentance, and sacramental confession, lest Spiritual Pride, like the dead elephant, fall and overwhelm you!

Pride blinds the eye, cripples new-born virtue, beats out acquired grace, and kills spiritual life.

Precaution II. Against Spiritual Pride the best safeguard is the constant practice of Humility.

"Be not high-minded, but fear. For if God spared not the natural branches, take heed lest He also spare not thee." (Rom. xi. 20, 21.)

Conclusion. In the Spiritual Combat, beware of dead elephants.

IV.

KNOWLEDGE OF SELF.

"*Ye say, We see; therefore your sin remaineth.*"—S. John ix. 41.

Introduction. In ancient times there existed in Greece a temple, and on its gate was inscribed in golden characters, KNOW THYSELF. When some one asked Plato why this inscription was there, he answered, "This is GOD's message to man: to know oneself is the most perfect knowledge."

Subject. *Self-knowledge.*

Point I. *The necessity of self-knowledge.* If we do not know our own condition, how can we ask GOD for what we want, not knowing what we want? we know not what are our temptations, our besetting sins; we may say we see, but in our blindness our sin remaineth. And when we pray, we pray vaguely, like babes crying, but not knowing what they cry for.

Point II. *The difficulty of self-knowledge.* Nothing is so deceitful as the heart; we blame in others what is most reprehensible in ourselves.

David, when Nathan came to him, was quite aware that he himself was a king, a prophet, a mighty man of war, a poet, a musician, and when he gave his sentence he flattered himself he was a just judge; but one thing he did not know, that he himself was a sinner, and that he had sinned worse than the man whose crime he denounced.

Absalom said to Hushai: "Is this thy kindness to thy friend? why wentest thou not with thy friend?" (2 Sam. xvi. 17.) He saw that the conduct of Hushai was to be reprehended, because he was not a true friend, but he forgot that he himself was a bad son, then in revolt against his father.

The Bishop of Laodicea. (Rev. iii. 17.) "Thou sayest, I am rich, and increased in goods, and have need of nothing, and knowest not that thou art wretched, and miserable, and poor, and blind, and naked.

Conclusion. "I counsel thee to buy of Me *gold* tried in the fire," the gold of burning, incorruptible charity, "that thou mayest be rich. And *white raiment*," remission of past sins, by absolution, so as to be re-clothed in innocence, "that thou mayest cover thy nakedness, and that the shame of thy nakedness do not appear; and anoint thine eyes with eye-salve"—the grace of the HOLY GHOST, opening the eyes to the knowledge of self and the sight of its blemishes, bringing sin to remembrance, "that thou mayest see."

V.

LITTLE SINS.

"*Dead flies cause the ointment of the apothecary to send forth a stinking savour.*"—Eccles. x. 1.

Introduction. Distinguish between venial sins and mortal sins. Mortal sins are those sins which are committed wilfully, knowing them to be sinful. Venial sins are those committed without premeditation, or without knowledge of their sinfulness. Venial sins are faults of infirmity, such as emotions of anger and impatience, exaggeration, flippant talk, wandering thoughts in prayer—in themselves little, but much in the aggregate.

Subject. *The importance of Little Sins.*

Point I. If we say we have no sin we deceive ourselves. This self-deception is very common; the sins are so light, so trifling, so little, that they are hardly noticed at the time, and are forgotten at the end of the day. Nevertheless they corrupt the ointment.

The clean, innocent heart, the heart that has been purified, is the pot of ointment, white and fragrant with good works, all that could be desired. Then in drops one fly, a little bit of impatience; then in falls another, a little thought of vanity; then a third, a feeling of obstinate adherence to one's own opinion; then a fourth, an emotion of disgust at having to fulfil a duty; then a fifth, the truth clipped at the edges;—and so on, one after another, in they fall, till the ointment is black instead of white, and the black faults corrupt the ointment, and it sends forth a stinking savour.

Remember, "For every idle word man will have to give account," and the wise man says, "He that despiseth small things shall fall by little and little."

Point II. Little sins persevered in prevent repentance; they produce a general habit of carelessness and indifference. Little faults pave the way to great ones. Little faults are committed so frequently, that their sinfulness is forgotten, and the sense of sin—the acute, moral sense, which should be always keen and clear—is blunted and dulled, and thus the consciousness of sin disappears, and therewith, readiness to repent.

Conclusion. The only way to be on your guard against these sins getting the mastery over you, corrupting the purity and simplicity of your heart, and deadening your moral sense, is to practise frequently and rigorously the duty of self-examination. Keep a watch, and mark these flies as they drop into the ointment, that you may pick them out every night when on your knees. Do not let these flies lie in the ointment till the morning, out with them at once, and so will you keep the ointment of divine grace in your hearts sweet smelling and pure, and meet to pour forth in unction upon the feet of your LORD.

VI.

THE GRACE OF GOD LEAVING A SINFUL SOUL.

"O the hope of Israel, the Saviour thereof in time of trouble, why shouldest Thou be as a stranger in the land, and as a wayfaring man that turneth aside to tarry for a night? . . . Yet Thou, O Lord, art in the midst of us, and we are called by Thy name; leave us not."—Jer. xiv. 8.

Subject. I wish to speak to you this day of the great fear we should have of suffering the grace of God to leave our souls, the great fear we should have of admitting sin to occupy the place in our souls which belongs of right to God.

I. It is impossible for God and Belial to possess the same heart; we cannot serve two masters, we must hold to the one and despise the other. I am going to illustrate the condition of the soul which, having possessed God and His grace, admits Satan and his sins to reign within it, by a passage of history.

When Absalom, the rebel, rose in arms against his father, king David, and marched to Jerusalem, "The king went forth and all the people after him, and tarried in a place that was far off," (2 Sam. xv. 17.) Jerusalem is desolate; its streets are empty; its market is deserted; no sound of steps in the marble palace; there is even no note of psalm swelling up in the temple. All is hushed. Look into the temple—the Levites are gone, the door-keepers, the singers, those who sounded the silver trumpets, those who prepared the sacrifices—all are gone. The temple is deserted. What is there to prevent the jackal and the hyæna entering and polluting the holy place? Look again. There, beside the ark of GOD stand the two priests, Zadok and Abiathar; as the golden cherubs stood and overshadowed it, so do these faithful priests of GOD and friends of David remain to protect the ark.

"And Absalom and all the people, the men of Israel, came to Jerusalem." At once the place is filled—the market is thronged, the palace floor is trodden—but by the enemies of David and of his GOD, the rebel and his host of rebels.

None remain in the city, true to David, save Zadok and Abiathar; and it was because they remained, that David was able to return once more, and resume his authority in Jerusalem.

II. Such is the incident narrated in Scripture. Let us see whether it may not be applied as a parable, so as to convey a moral lesson to our souls.

Jerusalem is man's body, in which divine grace dwells, "Ye are the temple of the HOLY GHOST which is in you;" and like a palace served by officers and attendants in due order and harmony, so in the body in which the Spirit dwells there are virtues attending on the Divine Presence,—*Love* sweetly regulating all in unity; *Joy* as master of the feast; *Peace* chief of the watch to prevent discord and broils; *Longsuffering* sitting as judge in the hall of justice; *Gentleness*, guardian over the prison; *Goodness*, keeper of the treasury; *Meekness*, steward among the servants; *Temperance*, chief butler. How beautiful is this picture.

But see! an Absalom arises, like a rebel son, the Flesh, or the Will; it revolts against the kingdom of the FATHER, and leads on a train of bad passions into the heart tenanted by the Grace of GOD. Immediately the Divine Presence is withdrawn, it flees, and tarries a long way off, with all the people—with all the virtues that formerly inhabited the man.

Then enters the rebel host, and finds the house "empty, swept, and garnished." Only Zadok and Abiathar remain: Zadok, *the knowledge of the truth*, and Abiathar, *the faculty of desiring better things;* and they sadly watch by the Ark of God, the indelible stamp, or character, impressed on every Christian at the Font.

Final Application. What a sad picture for angels to contemplate. Man fallen into the hands of his bad passions, given up to wayward lusts, led on by a rebel will. Faith sad and desponding; Hope faint and drooping, and the Christian sign forgotten and neglected.

Oh! is this a picture of any of you? Is the Will or the Flesh ruling in you, or is God sovereign? If your own Will or your own Passion sways you, leads you, governs you, then verily, God stands afar off with all His ministers. Call Him back, send forth Ahimaaz and Jonathan to the King, *i.e.* Prayer for pardon, and Prayer that He may return; and He will come unto you, and take up His abode with you, and dwell in you.

VII.

THE VALUE OF A SOUL.

"What is a man profited, if he shall gain the whole world, and lose his own soul? or what shall a man give in exchange for his soul?"—S. Matth. xvi. 26.

Introduction. In that wondrous story of the raising of the son of the widow of Nain, one sentence has often weighed upon me, and made me desire to know more—"He that was dead sat up, and began to speak."

What were the words that he uttered—his first exclamations on returning to life? He who had passed through the veil, and had traversed the valley of the shadow of death, he, to whom the mysteries beyond the tomb had been revealed. I have often wondered what was his first reflection on his return to earth. And it has struck me that in all probability it was something like this: "What is a man profited, if he shall gain the whole world, and lose his own soul? or what shall a man give in exchange for his soul?"

I. For consider: he now saw all things in their true value—he tested them by the light of eternity.

And how must this have influenced him in after life! Let us suppose a few instances.

He had been fond of pleasure before; now he sees the emptiness of pleasure.

He had been thoughtless before; now an earnestness takes possession of him.

He had been vain and conceited before; now he forgets what he is like.

Let us imagine a day in his life.

He strolls down the street and through the market—he sees the wrangling that goes on over a few farthings, and smiles; in the light of eternity how useless this immoderate expenditure of temper and energy?

He sees a child steal an apple from the stall, and he lays his hand on the child's arm and arrests him with an earnest look and the caution, "What is a man profited if he gain the whole world, and lose his own soul? Will you risk your eternal welfare for an apple?"

He looks in at the shop windows upon the ladies' dresses,

the silks, and satins, and velvets, trimmed and flounced, the head-gear, feathered and fantastic; and he says, "Oh, poor foolish women, to spend your thoughts on these trifles, instead of seeking the ornament of a meek and quiet spirit, which is in the sight of GOD of great price. What is a woman profited, if she shall gain a whole milliner's shop full of dresses, and lose her own soul?"

He finds two relations hating each other for a piece of inheritance, a patch of land of no great value and size; and he says, "Why this hostility among relatives? seek peace and ensue it. What is a man profited if he gets half a dozen acres of grass-land, and loses his own soul?"

He finds a litigation going on between neighbouring farmers about a right of way; so much money spent in law, so much heart-burning, such hard and malicious speeches, that he exclaims, "What is a man profited if he gets a thoroughfare over a bit of weedy common, and loses his own soul?"

He sees his mother troubled at a bit of gossip got up by the neighbours, that she is looking out to be married again. She is troubled and in tears—it is not true, it is unkind. What does the young man say? "Mother, let not these things trouble you; what matters it if people speak evil of you, and false things are reported; time is short, eternity is long. There will be no gossiping and slander hereafter."

II. Now I wish you to lay this to heart. It is quite possible for you to learn to view everything, as did that young man, in the light of eternity. If we live the life of faith, so that the future is to us a reality, then, at once, the transitoriness, the insufficiency, the vanity of the things of time, become most evident to us. Yes, we can see things just as did that young man, if we will only try. And chief of all, let the value of the soul be remembered,—that everything may be weighed against that; that the question may always be, Will this profit my soul? or will this harm my soul? My soul is very precious, it is breathed into me by GOD, it is a part of the Divine essence, it is redeemed by JESUS CHRIST at the price of His most precious blood.

Conclusion. O teach me, LORD, now to know the value of my soul, that I spend not my life in grasping after that which cannot satisfy, or in giving my soul's welfare in exchange for what can only endure for a brief season.

VIII.

REST IN CHRIST.

"*The dove found no rest for the sole of her foot, and she returned unto him in the ark, for the waters were on the face of the whole earth: then he put forth his hand, and took her, and pulled her in unto him into the ark.*"—Gen. viii. 9.

Introduction. May be the dove had pined for freedom, had felt the restraint of the ark. The raven had gone forth, why not she?

Then the window was opened, she spread her wings and was free. She darted where she listed, over the rippling blue waters, flashing in the sun, through the sweet cool air, and all was well for a time. At length she was hungry, and *she sought food. There was none.*

Then she wearied. Night approached, the wind freshened, the waves rose, the brine splashed over her, her plumes were draggled; she was exhausted, she could fly no more, and clouds gathered for a storm. *She sought a place of rest. There was none.*

Then the setting sun stared over the scene from the west, and as it went down, in its eye was the Ark. She saw it. Hope, joy, confidence revived,—there was food and there was rest; she sped like an arrow to the goal, the window was opened, and she was taken in.

Subject I. *The soul strayed from the Church.*

May be some poor soul has felt the restraint in the Church, or it has craved for something different, some novelty; and it deserts.

All goes well at first,—it is stimulated and excited, the novelty pleases, its liberty delights it; but when all this palls, when it wants *food*—can it get that? No! in the Church alone is the Body of Jesus, the food which alone can satisfy the craving of the soul.

And again it seeks *rest.* Is there rest in the shifting opinions of men? in the theories and doctrines of to-day, which change as the moon? No. In the Church alone is there Certainty on which faith can rest, for she has been assured infallibility by the promise of God.

Then the poor strayed soul comes back, and is taken in once more, and feeds on Christ, Who is her strength, and sustenance, and life, and cleaves to and reposes on that faith which was once for all delivered to the saints.

Subject II. *The soul lost in sin.*

Let us take the dove now as the baptized soul flying to sin, and trying to find in that food and rest.

Food! all is soiled and sodden in the water. Take anything that the world can give, and try to make that the food of the immortal soul, and the soul will turn away from it with loathing.

The soul was not made for that. Business . . . Pleasure . . . Ambition . . . Love. All things necessary or well enough in their way, good enough in their place, but not as food for the soul. Let it try—there is a craving still.

Rest! all is floating and shifting, nothing remains and endures. And the soul which is eternal needs something which is eternal on which it can repose. Relatives are taken away; home changes; friendships are broken up; that to which we cling now, drifts from our grasp to-morrow; that to which we held yesterday has floated from our reach to-day.

Conclusion. *The return of the soul.*

At last, may be, the soul recognises that this world cannot satisfy its desires, cannot give it an enduring and sure repose; and it turns to the Ark, turns to its own true home. And lo! the pierced hands are put forth in absolution,—it is taken in with joy, and it rests on the heart of JESUS, and feeding on His sacred Body finds satisfaction, and in the everlasting arms finds rest. Food that indeed fills the heart, rest that indeed is sweet, till the Ark strands on the heavenly Zion, and the door is opened for the soul to fly in freedom, in satisfaction, and in confidence through the new heavens over the regenerate earth.

IX.

THE SWEETENED WATERS.

"*And when they came to Marah they could not drink of the waters of Marah, for they were bitter. . . . . And Moses cried unto the Lord; and the Lord showed him a tree, which when he had cast into the waters, the waters were made sweet.*"—Exod. xv. 23, 25.

Introduction. A narration of the circumstances.

Application I. And to how many of us, entering on the wilderness of this life full of devious paths, *is not the water bitter?*

We drink of pleasure, for a little while, may be, it delights; but then comes the gall in our mouths, and we turn away in disgust.

We try the world's applause—at first it, too, pleases; but then at last its utter hollowness, its venality, its unreality, its dishonesty, strike us, and the gall is on our lips.

We try earthly love—it is sweet at first, say it be an honest love, but one entirely of earth, not rooted first in GOD, and then after a while, little by little, the bitter springs up between the teeth.

Hear Solomon:—Eccles. II. (read).

Well, the people murmured at Marah, so do we. Those whom the disappointment of life embitters become misanthropes, retire in disgust and sullen animosity into themselves, till they hate even themselves.

Application II. *But look up!* Is there not a tree casting its shadow over the land, a tree whose leaves are for the healing of the nations?

It is the Cross. Cast that into your bitter pool, and lo! the waters are sweetened.

I glory in infirmities, said S. Paul; could he have said that, had not the cross sweetened them to him?

The Cross in mental anguish. Are you in distress of mind, that most bitter of all waters to drink? Cast in the Cross. Call to mind the mental anguish of JESUS in Gethsemane, when His sweat was as great drops of blood falling down to the ground. Unite your sufferings to His, and the waters are sweet.

The Cross in bodily pain. This again is a bitter pool of which to drink, to be tortured night and day, and find no rest; the fevered blood, the wrung nerves, the aching head, the weary bones, what more bitter? Look up to JESUS on the Cross, suffering His agony, racked, bleeding, bruised. Unite your bodily sufferings to His—once more the waters are sweet.

The Cross in loss of friends. Another bitter pool, making the heart turn to gall. But remember Him whose friend Lazarus died, whose friend Peter denied Him, whose friend Judas betrayed Him; Him who was deserted in the garden by all His friends; who when He died had not His friends to gather round His death-bed, for "they stood afar off." Unite your sense of bereavement to His—once again the gall turns to honey.

The Cross in poverty. That also is as wormwood, depressing the heart, filling the mind with anxiety, the soul with despair. But who is He that had not where to lay His head, who was ministered to of the substance of some poor women, who was stripped of all at the last, who was beholden to charity for a grave? Unite your poverty to the poverty of JESUS, and the waters have changed their taste, the Tree has healed them.

Conclusion. Lo! the true Moses, even JESUS, leads you on from the bitter waters to Elim, having proved you at the pool. Elim, the place of twelve wells and threescore and ten palm trees, where you may encamp, and encamping find rest. The twelve wells are the apostles, and the seventy palm trees are His disciples, now planted in security, now flowing with gladness, in the Eden of GOD.

X.

THE CHURCH TRIED.

"*And when the sun was going down, a deep sleep fell upon Abram; and lo, an horror of great darkness fell upon him . . . . and it came to pass, that when the sun went down, and it was dark, behold, a smoking furnace, and a burning lamp that passed between those pieces.*"—Gen. xv. 12, 17.

Introduction. This passage describes the first vision recorded in Holy Scripture. The circumstances introducing it, and accompanying it, are remarkable.

Abram was on his way back from the rescue of Lot, and had received the blessing of Melchizedek. GOD appeared to him, and made him a promise that he should have a son, and seed as the stars of heaven and the sand on the seashore.

This promise was accompanied by a prophecy that his seed should be afflicted and be in bondage, but that it should be delivered from its bondage undestroyed.

First Signification of the Vision. The *lamp* in the vision represented the people of Israel illumined by GOD's abiding presence. "The light of Israel shall be for a fire, and his Holy One for a flame." (Isa. x. 17.) "The LORD shall be to thee an everlasting light." (Isa. lx. 19.)

The lamp moved *between the pieces* of the sacrifice Abram had prepared. This was a token of covenant.

The lamp entered *the Furnace;* that is, the iron furnace of Egypt (Deut. iv. 20) where the people of Israel was tried with the fire of affliction.

The people passed through that furnace, but were not destroyed by it, they were "persecuted, but not forsaken, cast down, but not destroyed."

Second Signification of the Vision. But this was not all. The vision was written for our admonition, upon whom the ends of the world are come.

Once more a *covenant* has been made, not with the blood of bulls and calves, and the ashes of an heifer, but with the blood of JESUS. And this is the covenant: "Lo, I am with you always, even unto the end of the world;" "This generation shall not pass away till all be fulfilled;" "Upon this rock will I build My Church, and the gates of hell shall not prevail against it." This is the covenant: that the seed of CHRIST, the spiritual generation, shall be as the stars for multitude, that it shall possess the land.

The history of the Jewish Church foreshadows the history of the Christian Church. The Catholic Church is now the *lamp.* CHRIST is in it by His power and authority. "Whosoever receiveth you receiveth Me;" and above all by His Sacramental Presence.

The Church, like the lamp, *moves;* it is ever in progress, never stationary, and she moves ever nearer to the *furnace* of affliction and persecution.

The Israelites were wanderers in the land, then were received into court favour, and were established by the state in Egypt; and then the third stage came, persecution by the state which no longer knew Joseph. So with the Church, once a wanderer and needy she was received by religious kings, and exalted to a position of established prosperity. Now comes the stage when kings all over Europe arise which know not Joseph, and with them comes persecution.

The vision of the Apocalypse unfolds the same history, and S. Paul and S. Peter sound the alarm note to warn us that, once more, "Kings of the earth will stand up, and the rulers take counsel together against the Lord and against His Christ."

Application I. The dangers apprehended are, a wide-spread infidelity, a pretence of religion without dogma, an apostasy from the doctrine of the Incarnation, a disbelief in the supernatural, culminating in open and cruel persecution.

Already we feel the hot breath of the furnace, and we know that the Church is approaching those flames. Look! dim and feeble seems the lamp, its brightness is obscured, its sides blurred with many a stain, its wick untrimmed, its oil clogged with dust. Frail and unprepared it passes into the furnace!

Look! the fire roars around it, the hungry flames leap up, the coals glow under it, volumes of smoke roll around it. Falteringly it advances, now hidden from our sight by the black vapours, now by the lurid glare of the fire, but it is there still, like a tiny white star, calm and steady in those tossing waves of flame.

Look! the coals crash about it, and a column of sparks rises to the black heavens, the furnace is ruined—can the lamp survive? Yes! look once more, brightening and whitening, moving still, gathering brilliancy, it emerges from the furnace, and the ashes turn cold and dead before its growing splendour, and the flames fall and die out.

Application II. What is said of the Church is said of each one of you. You are entered into covenant with GOD, and you also must be tried.

Fear, I say, if all goes smooth, if you have no temptation, no conflict to wage, if the world smiles, duty seems easy—then all is not safe—fear, I say, fear then.

But *fear not* if the furnace is hot, and you struggle with the flames, fear not if temptation and trial surround you, it is a pledge of your covenant.

"The LORD is my light and my salvation; whom then shall I fear? the LORD is the strength of my life; of whom then shall I be afraid? When the wicked, even mine enemies and my foes, came upon me to eat up my flesh, they stumbled and fell. Though an host of men were laid against me, yet shall not my heart be afraid: and though there rose up war against me, yet will I put my trust in Him." (Ps. xxvii. 1—3.)

XI.

THE PILGRIMAGE OF LIFE.

"*Though I walk through the valley of the shadow of death, I will fear no evil: for Thou art with me, Thy rod and Thy staff they comfort me.*"—Ps. xxiii. 4.

Introduction. I think there is something wondrously touching in the thought of David, the shepherd boy, singing these words whilst sitting on a wild thyme bank, crook in hand, watching his father's flock, in all the glory of an eastern sunset. Perhaps it was growing late, and the yellow western sky flamed with the last glories of departing day. From the woods sounded the howls of the beasts of prey, awaking to their work, ready to issue from the shadows of the trees, the lion roaring after his prey, the jackal following in his traces.

As he hears these hungry voices, he looks to his sheep, and thinks, Well! they are secure, for I am here to defend them; and then, meditating on his own condition as one of GOD's flock and the sheep of His pasture, he exclaims: "The LORD is my shepherd, therefore can I lack nothing." He knows that he loves his own sheep, and that he will lead them into pleasant pastures and by running streams, therefore he adds, "He shall feed me in a green pasture, and lead me forth beside the waters of comfort." And then he sees how his sheep are inclined to stray, and he runs and guides them back into places of safety, therefore he says: "He shall convert my soul, and bring me forth into the paths of righteousness." And now he drives his flock home, they descend the valley where the cold shadow is fallen, and the white fog has begun to form over the brook, and he exclaims, "Though I walk through the valley of the shadow of death, I will fear no evil."

And lastly, as he folds his sheep in safety, and reviews his watchfulness and care of them through the day, he sings: "But Thy loving-kindness and mercy shall follow me all the days of my life: and I will dwell in the house of the LORD for ever."

Subject. Such is David's song. I will not take the whole of it, but comment solely on the words of my text.

The *valley of the shadow of death* is—

1. This life.

2. Death.

It is this life, because it is under the *shadow* of death. From the moment we enter this world that shadow lies on us. Of a child born into this world you can predict nothing, whether it will be great or insignificant, rich or poor, happy or sad, save this one thing—it will surely die.

And now what is given us in this valley to be our comfort and stay? The *rod* and the *staff*—the rod to correct, the staff to support.

The Rod of God chastises us when we would wander, it is laid on us as the cross which we are to bear; it is often heavy, it is always salutary; it often seems an evil, it always is a good. When anything rises to afflict us, to cross our wills, to disappoint our expectations, to frustrate our hopes, to check our impatience, do not let us chafe and beat against the barrier, it is the rod of God held out to keep us from straying, and to guide us into the right way.

The Staff of God supports us when we are feeble. Without that staff what should we do, to what should we cling? In weakness, in exhaustion, in mistrust of self, in consciousness of backsliding, out goes the hand, the staff is planted firm, and we clutch at it, and our feet are strengthened, and we are able to stand. Not only so, but when we have fallen and have no power to rise, that staff is our comfort still, for to that we cling, and by that we lift up ourselves.

And now, in conclusion, let us take the breathings of a pious and timorous soul expressing its fears to God, and let us hear the answer of God to that poor soul; let us take it as David may have imagined it, and with that we shall conclude.

Colloquy. *Pilgrim.* O my God! I have a long journey before me, and I know not the road—whither shall I go?

Master. I will bring thee forth into the paths of righteousness.

P. O my LORD! perils environ me, the savage lion walking about seeking whom he may devour. I am unarmed and weak, and I shall fall a ready prey; the thieves also are ready to strip me, and wound me, and leave me half dead and naked by the way.

M. Fear not, My son; My lovingkindness and protection shall follow thee all the days of thy life.

P. But, gracious LORD! the journey is beyond my strength; I shall faint with thirst, and hunger, and exhaustion of body.

M. My son, thou shalt go on from strength to strength; the pools shall be filled with water; I will anoint thine head with oil, prepare a table for thee in the wilderness, and thy cup shall be full.

P. O, dear Master, see! I stand upon the brink of the valley, and the river flows cold, and grey, and ghastly below. I fear!

M. When thou passest through the waters, I am with thee.

P. Master! the chill of the wave of death has reached me; I am horribly afraid, the wave goes over me.

M. My son, I give thee My rod and staff to comfort thee.

Oh! the retrospect from the fold when Jordan is passed, and the Promised Land is won. Surely then the cry will be, "Thy lovingkindness and mercy have followed me all the days of my life; and now will I dwell in the house of the LORD for ever."

XII.

PREPARATION FOR DEATH.

"*What meanest thou, O sleeper? arise, call upon thy God.*"—Jonah i. 6.

Introduction. A furious storm had fallen on the vessel; the deep worked as a churn; the ship plunged, ungoverned by the helm, in the yeasty flood; the sailors cast out their wares and lightened the vessel; the fish gathered around the vessel, waiting for its wreck, that they might feed upon the dead.

And where was Jonah? In the sides of the vessel, fast asleep. The ship-master went to him and cried, "What meanest thou, O sleeper? arise and call upon thy God."

Subject. And you—may not you be like Jonah? in imminent peril of death, a plank between you and eternity? I come then to you—you so careless, so drowsy, nay, so sound asleep in your security, that I may shake you like that ship-master, and shout in your ears, "What meanest thou, O sleeper? arise and call upon thy God."

Point I. *Death may be near at hand.*

Are you in the least aware that death may come to you at any moment? I quite allow that you admit it tacitly; but I do not believe that you realise it clearly. And yet death is armed against old and young. This is how David describes him: "He hath drawn his sword, he hath bent his bow, and made ready the instruments of death." His sword is drawn against those who are near, his arrows are for those who are afar off. The sword for the aged, the bow for the young.

And then the instruments of death. How many they are, and in what variety. A suit of wet clothes, through which you catch a chill and fever; a ladder, from which your foot slips, and you fall; a horse which throws you; a rusty nail which poisons the blood; a little breath of air laden with the seeds of typhus—seeds so minute that you cannot see them through any lens yet constructed; a crumbling stone by the side of a canal. Oh! there are numbers of instruments in the hand of death; indeed, death seems to grasp at anything that lies ready and use that, be it what it may; and we often wonder at the strange instruments he uses.

And what is more, there is no avoiding them. Let us follow him at his work. There, he drops a little seed of cholera into that pool. The water sinks into the ground and carries that minute spore with it by underground channels into that drain, and the drain conducts it into yonder stream, and the stream washes it down; it passes this cluster of houses, and that village, and it goes along its way imperceptible to all. But there, from that cottage is a girl coming out with a tin can to fetch water; the tiny seed is moving on—will it pass before she dips the can? No, she dips at the instant it is there, and the seed is taken, quite unknown by her, to the cottage. Will she drink? She hesitates, and without knowing why, declines. But her father comes in at that moment, hot and tired; he takes up the can—ah! every bullet has got its billet!—the seed has fallen where it was destined to fall. To-morrow the man is dead.

Point II. *Preparation for Death necessary.*

And now, if this be so, how can there be such a disregard of death?

I see one heaping up sin upon sin, and saying, Oh, there is time enough, I will repent at my leisure.

What meanest thou, O sleeper? arise and call upon thy God.

I see one greedy of gain, gathering to himself treasures, scrupling not at the means whereby he accumulates money, so long as he may make money.

What meanest thou, O sleeper? arise and call upon thy God.

I see one with opportunities of serving God before him—the church bell calling, the altar spread—but all opportunities systematically neglected.

What meanest thou, O sleeper? arise and call upon thy God.

I see one given wholly to pleasure, with no thought save how self may be gratified, the senses tickled, the time passed—a butterfly life, a profitless life.

What meanest thou, O sleeper? arise and call upon thy God.

Conclusion. Arise and call upon thy God, arise from thy lethargy, from thy sin, from thy vanities, from thy self-seeking; arise even from thy necessary business; arise and call upon thy God to forgive thee that which is past, to make thee decline from sin and incline to righteousness, that death may not come upon thee unawares. "Awake, thou that sleepest, and arise from the dead, and Christ shall give thee light."

XIII.

THE WATERS OF GRACE.

"*Behold, waters issued out from under the threshold of the house eastward . . . And when the man that had the line in his hand went forth eastward, he measured a thousand cubits, and he brought me through the waters; the waters were to the ancles. Again he measured a thousand, and brought me through the waters; the waters were to the knees. Again he measured a thousand, and brought me through; the waters were to the loins. Afterwards he measured a thousand; and it was a river that I could not pass over; for the waters were risen, waters to swim in, a river that could not be passed over.*"—Ezek. xlvii. 1—5.

Introduction. Ezekiel has been describing the constitution of the Church as a city built upon CHRIST, the rock; in figure he has foretold its ministry, its sacraments, and its privileges; and now he, under a striking symbol, unfolds the mystery of Grace.

Subject. *The Interpretation of this Symbol.*

Point I. The river of the water of life is often spoken of in Holy Scripture. It is this that CHRIST promised to the woman of Samaria: "Whosoever drinketh of the water that I shall give him, shall never thirst; but the water that I shall give him shall be in him a well of water springing up into everlasting life." It is the water of that river alluded to by David, that shall "make glad the city of GOD," the "river of the water of life, pure as crystal, proceeding out of the throne of GOD and of the Lamb," seen in vision by S. John.

And what is meant by the waters? The Grace of GOD, ever flowing, pure and sparkling; it *cleanses* the sinner from his defilement, first, in baptism, from original sin; then in absolution, from post-baptismal sin.

It *refreshes* the weary, renews their strength, flowing out of the House of GOD in the Sacraments of strength.

Point II. What is meant by the measurements of its depth? This represents to us GOD'S grace as exhibited in the history of the Church, and of ourselves.

First, it flowed, a little stream out of the side of CHRIST, that east gate of the Temple of His Body, and but a few were numbered with the elect; then it spread, and its depth increased, as nation after nation became Christian; and lastly, it cannot be passed over, in the immeasurable perfection of the final glory of CHRIST'S kingdom.

But to ourselves it has a further meaning.

First, it reaches our ancles, as we enter the stream of grace as little infants, admitted into CHRIST'S favour, and made partakers of His goodness, in Holy Baptism. Then we try the flood in Confirmation, and it reaches to our knees. Again in Communion, and it flows about our waists. Again and again we enter, and often we lave ourselves in that blessed stream, and ever it seems more refreshing, and ever it seems to deepen, till at last we find it "waters to swim in, a river that cannot be passed over."

Conclusion. And now, to conclude, there is one practical lesson I wish to impress upon you from this vision, and that is, from the measuring, before the waters were entered. I wish you to observe that the angel who was with Ezekiel always measured a thousand, before he suffered the prophet to enter the stream, and be sensible of an increase of volume and depth in the waters. I wish you then to learn this. If you would also find Divine Grace flow for you in increased abundance, roll in a deeper tide, *measure before you enter it.*

That is, examine and prove yourselves by the scale of GOD's law, examine and prove whether you have made any advance, whether you have gone, not a thousand paces forward, but one or two, or three, even.

Without that careful measuring, and without that advance, the waters of Divine Grace will not rise, and you will have to learn a new lesson, if ever you are to find them "waters to swim in, a river that could not be passed over."

XIV.

THE UNHEALED MARSHES.

"*He said unto me, These waters issue out toward the east country, and go down into the desert, and go into the sea: which, being brought forth into the sea, the waters shall be healed. And it shall come to pass, that everything that liveth, which moveth, whithersoever the rivers shall come, shall live: and there shall be a very great multitude of fish, because these waters shall come hither: for they shall be healed; and every thing shall live whither the river cometh. . . . But the miry places thereof and the marishes thereof shall not be healed; they shall be given to salt.*"—Ezek. xlvii. 8, 9, 11.

Introduction. Ezekiel is describing the effect of Divine Grace. The sea into which the river flows is the Dead Sea, the sea which lay over the accursed cities, on which a judgment brooded.

It is an image of the Gentile world, lying in wickedness, stagnant, and corrupt, and putrifying; civilization bad and decaying through its licentiousness; civil order rotten and falling to pieces; philosophy degenerated into Epicureanism; religion a mass of corrupting fables; nothing life-giving, nothing purifying, nothing renovating. Then the rill of pure water enters, the blessed revelation of JESUS CHRIST—first a brook and then a river, gradually purifying and giving life, so that "whithersoever the rivers shall come, everything that liveth, which moveth, shall live."

Point I. But it has a further meaning. *The dead sea is the human heart.*

Into that, Divine Grace enters, and by little and little it purges and purifies it, so that by the river bank "shall grow all trees for meat, whose leaf shall not fade, neither shall the fruit thereof be consumed, because the waters issued out of the sanctuary" (verse 12.)

Virtues shall spring up; all that did live, the natural elements of good, shall live and grow with new vigour, and in addition supernatural graces shall spring up and flourish with unfading leaf and unconsumed fruit, "because the waters issued out of the sanctuary."

This then is the work of divine grace in the heart *purifying* and *giving life.* It purifies it of its evil and corruption, of its death and decay; it vivifies its natural good and infuses supernatural virtue.

Point II. *But the miry places and marishes are not healed.*

What then are the places which remain salt, these places where the pure crystal water cannot circulate, and in circulating, give life and renovation?

The miry places and marishes are the unstable, the uncertain souls that endure for a season, but in time of temptation fall away; those who are good and Church-going because it is respectable, those who are steady, only because not tempted, those who are Catholics, only because the services are nicer than in Protestant places of worship, those who are without any solid foundation of principle—weak and fluctuating in their desires, not resolute in will, not earnest in religion, who show a green surface of profession—plenty of display of godliness, bowing, and crossing, and Church-going, and talk of religion—but who have no bottom to their character.

These are they who come to Church to show off their bonnets or see each other's faces; these are they who are ready to serve God when there is pleasure, and profit, and praise to be got out of it, who will keep all the feasts, but not a single fast; who are utterly unreliable persons when trial arises, or their self-will is crossed, their self-love is ruffled, their self-esteem is not flattered.

Conclusion. The parish priest knows plenty of these, and knows by sad experience too, how true it is that "the miry places and marshes shall not be healed."

XV.

THE BUILDING OF BABEL.

"*And they said, Go to, let us build us a city and a tower, whose top may reach unto heaven; and let us make us a name, lest we be scattered abroad upon the face of the whole earth.*"—Gen. xi. 4.

Introduction The history of the building of Babel, and the confounding of the language.

Subject. There is many a Babel building going on still. Man indeed is ever building Babels of some sort, that he may make him a name, and reach heaven by his own ways. Babels these are which are indeed confusion, Babels left unfinished, whose builders are scattered ere the tower reaches heaven. There are religious Babels and worldly Babels; Babels, that is, to reach heaven, and Babels for the making of a name. I will speak of both.

Point I. *Religious Babels.*

Religious schemes fail often because the object is worldly. Collection lists are printed, great names head it, there are boards of managers and committees to see to the carrying out of the philanthropic ends, and the whole fails, or fails to effect all that was desired;—why? Because the love of GOD was not the foundation on which it was built.

Take also the religious bodies of sectarians. Whence have they arisen? "Go to, let us build us a city and a tower, whose top may reach unto heaven." Men, pious in their intention, but mistaken, break away from the unity of the Church, to build Babels of their own, to reach unto heaven. And with what result? confusion reigns amongst them. Is not dissent everywhere a scene of division, of breaking up and scattering? whereas everywhere the Church is drawing together towards closer unity. There was a good intent in the founder, but GOD has looked out of heaven and confounded the builders, because the foundations were not laid by Him on the unshaken Rock.

Point II. *Worldly Babels.*

You surely know of some such. Accumulation of fortune, "let us make us a name;" the making of a family, the securing of a position in society, in the literary, or scientific, or political world. The making a dash in society, the building up a splendid future through present thrift—these crumble away, or the builders are scattered. The parent has amassed a fortune, and bought a country residence that he may make his family, and the son runs through his income and disappears. Great and costly efforts have been made by entertainments, and the like, to keep up with society, and in a moment their failure becomes manifest, and the worthlessness of the friends, bought at such a price, transpires.

Conclusion. Let each examine his own work, and weigh

well whether he is giving his time, his thoughts, his energies, to building what is a Babel, and which will end in disappointment and confusion.

XVI.

THE BUILDING OF JERUSALEM.

"*Behold, I lay in Zion for a foundation a stone, a tried stone, a precious corner-stone, a sure foundation.*"—Isa. xxviii. 16.

Introduction. The tower of Babel was erected in time of tranquillity. Jerusalem was rebuilt in time of war. When Babel was built, everything needed was at hand; when Jerusalem was rebuilt, the builders were destitute of all. When Babel was built, the princes favoured the undertaking; the rebuilding of Jerusalem was opposed by the nobles. But Babel failed, Jerusalem was finished.

Subject. *Jerusalem is a figure of the Church.*

All her members are stones built into her, to form a glorious habitation for the LORD. This is the "city which hath foundations, whose builder and maker is GOD."

Point I. Such, then, is the Church, founded by our LORD JESUS CHRIST. Her belief was taught her by JESUS CHRIST; her sacraments were instituted by JESUS CHRIST; her ministry was commissioned by JESUS CHRIST. Everything in the Church is of JESUS, comes from Him, is of Him, lives by Him. It is He who teaches us through His Word, it is He who speaks with authority through His ministry, it is He who touches us through His sacraments.

And the Church is built up stage by stage, notwithstanding persecution, opposition, disfavour, deficiency of means; it is built up on the changeless foundation.

For eighteen hundred years that work has been going on, stone on stone has been laid, tower after tower has risen, and the ramparts are being set up in order.

Look at the history of the Church, and see if it be possible to doubt that it is the counterpart to Jerusalem, that it is the LORD's own city.

For eighteen hundred years it has gone on increasing, from a handful to a great multitude. It was the Church which converted England when it was the abode of savages, it is the Church which has remained through all these hundreds of years one in faith; and why?

Point II. Because CHRIST promised that His Church should last for ever; because whatsoever is of His doing cannot be undone, whatsoever is built on His foundation cannot be overthrown, whatsoever is protected by His assurance Satan and man cannot destroy.

Can this be said of other communities, founded by men, built on their opinion, sustained only by their exertions? That which is human is perishable, that which is divine must endure eternally.

Conclusion. Now, why was it Jerusalem was built, but the building of Babel failed—that in spite of all disadvantages Jerusalem was a success, and in spite of all advantages Babel was a failure?

Because the motive which actuated the builders of Jerusalem was zeal for the glory of GOD; the motive of the builders of Babel, on the other hand, was the love of self.

My brethren, there is a lesson here—you see what work will endure, and what work will fail. Work for GOD, that work will last. Work for self, that work will come to nought, to desolation.

XVII.

THE ARK OF THE CHURCH.

"*The waters increased and bare up the ark.*"—Gen. vii. 17.

Introduction. The ark is a type of the Church. Description of the ruin of the cities and towers, and the submergence of the mountains by the rising flood. And in all this ruin of great cities, this destruction of strong citadels, this overthrow of great peoples, of course that frail vessel containing Noah and his family perished? No!

Subject. *The waters increased and bare up the ark.* That in few words is the history of the Church. The waters have risen and wrecked nations, the waters have risen and raged against the Church—the waters have risen and swept away civilization, but as they increased, "they bare up the ark."

I. The persecutions of the Emperors of Rome against Christianity, the stake, the sword, the rack, the chain, all cruelty could devise, used against the Church, that poor feeble little body of poor illiterate men and women, but "*the waters increased and bare up the ark.*"

II. The heresies of Arius, Nestorius, Pelagius, &c. Persecution raged before, now it is error spreads everywhere, false belief in the nature of CHRIST, and in the responsibility of man. Error in the palace, error in the streets of the city, error in the schools, error in some instances flowing in through the joints of the vessel, and corrupting the bishops: surely the Church must sink! But no, "*the waters increased and bare up the ark.*"

III. Then came the invasion of the Teutonic barbarians.

The world was swept by savage hordes, the old treasures of ancient civilization sank under the flood of brute ignorance that rushed over Europe; in Europe civilization, and with it Christianity, seemed to go down before the Teuton; in the East civilization, and with it Christianity, seemed to go down before the Mohammedan. But no! regeneration rose out of the ruin. The Teuton hordes were tamed and baptized; the Eastern Church conquered Russia and northern Asia. "*The waters increased and bare up the ark.*"

IV. And now another flood rises and threatens. It is not expiring Heathenism, it is not Heresy, it is not Brutality, it is Modern Doubt.

That is our great peril now. Three hundred years ago Luther, Zwingli, Calvin, Bucer, and the rest of the reformers taught men to *doubt:* and doubt, which began with a few articles of the Christian faith has gone on till it includes all. This is essentially the era of doubt—doubt in the truth of Revelation, in the inspiration of Scripture, in future punishment of the ungodly; doubt of the sacred obligations of morality, of the efficacy of prayer; doubt of the existence of a soul, of the Divinity of CHRIST.

It would seem as if this terrible outbreak of doubt, swelling like a flood and threatening the Church, must engulf her! But no, as the waters increase, the ark will be borne aloft.

Conclusion. Finally let us learn to cleave with heart and soul to the Church of CHRIST, there alone is safety; trust in her, for she is built by CHRIST, fear not for her, she is protected of GOD.

XVIII.

THE BURNING BUSH.

"*The bush burned with fire, and the bush was not consumed.*"—Exod. iii. 2.

Introduction. Narrate the circumstances.

The signification was gradually unfolded; as in most of the other visions, it has a reference, first, to the then condition of Israel, and an ulterior one to the Catholic Church.

First Signification. *The Bush is the Israelitish people,* a thorn-bush full of prickles, a tangled, ragged mass of dry branches, a scrubby, unseemly plant.

Such was the chosen people; a nation perverse, stiff-necked, going two ways, rebellious and insincere.

Nevertheless, GOD was in the midst of them, enduring their perversity, gently bearing with their stiff-neckedness, compassionating them—not consuming them.

Second Signification. *The Bush is the Christian Church,* full of deficiences, blemishes, perversities, apparent evil, base worldliness, neglect of duty, disregard of GOD, and yet, in the midst of that thorn-bush, GOD is present without consuming it.

He is present even here! Here in this Church, here, in the midst of us with our shortcomings, our self-seeking, our pride, our vanity, our carelessness. He is here, and He consumes us not.

Third Signification. *The Bush is Man.* In the midst of our temptations, afflictions, and the trials besetting each one of us, O my brother! in that daily round of work, with the thorns of care thrusting this way and that, in the stir of business, the tangle of trade, the strife of tongues, GOD may be present, present in His sacramental union with us, present as our defence against the world and against ourselves, present to enlighten and to comfort, but not to consume.

XIX.

THE PERSON OF JESUS CHRIST.

"*This is eternal life: that they may know Thee, the only true God, and Jesus Christ, Whom Thou hast sent.*"—S. John xvii. 3.

Introduction. Man is given by GOD a free will; he can serve GOD, or refuse to serve Him, as he likes. GOD made man to be happy; man can only be happy by obeying GOD. GOD seeks to bring man to obedience, not by constraint, for that would destroy his free will, but by gaining his love. How gain man's love, but by an exhibition of His own love? How best exhibit His love? By becoming incarnate, so that man may have a proof of GOD's love to him, and may have in the GOD-Man a person whom to love.

I. *God is not an idea.* The philosophers of old and modern times argue the existence of GOD, demonstrate Him, that they may believe in Him; and this is all well for a rational man. But man cannot wait till he has proved GOD to his satisfaction, till he finds GOD at the end of a sum, the result of a syllogism; he must have GOD the object of his affection. The heathen had GOD as an idea, and the idea was impracticable, it failed. They did not keep GOD's law, for they had first to demonstrate that there was a GOD, then that He had a law, and then to find out what the law was, and death came before the discovery was made. It was too long a business. Man must have God to start from, not God to work up to.

II. *God is a Person.* Yes, Jesus Christ is God and Man, a human Person and also a Divine Person—the divine and human personality in one. The Catholic reaches the mark at once; whilst the deist is demonstrating that there is a God, the Christian child believes in Him; what the heathen philosopher crept towards, and just touched as he dropped into his grave, the Christian infant starts learning it at its mother's knee.

Whilst the philosopher discusses God's nature, the Christian child has learned to love Him, and has kissed the cross, and feels that God is love.

Whilst the philosopher is finding out God's laws, the Christian child is observing them.

To the philosopher it is a life's labour to lay the foundation; the Christian has his laid, and his life's labour is to build thereupon.

III. *What sort of person.* I will tell you what sort of person is Jesus, the God-Man, Him whom we love.

He is a child obedient to His mother, a lad working in the shop, loving the Temple, weary at the well, pleading for His murderers, deserted by His friends.

A Person full of love, full of tenderness, full of sorrows.

A Person tempted like me, tried like me, suffering like me—therefore a Person Whom I can love.

Not One Who *was* merely, but One Who *was, and is, and is to be;* Who was Man, Who is Man, and Who will be Man through all eternity.

Conclusion. Come then! try to love Him by an act of

free will, and loving Him you will fulfil the law, for you will readily keep it out of love; and keeping it you will find happiness, and finding happiness, you will accomplish the will of your Creator.

XX.

ON SPIRITUAL ADVANCE.

"*And the Lord said unto Moses, Wherefore criest thou unto Me? speak unto the children of Israel, that they go forward.*"—Exod. xiv. 15.

Introduction. Narration of the circumstances. The perplexity of the Israelites without weapons of defence; the sea before, the foe behind. They murmur. Moses is in despair. All hope seems lost. Then comes that wondrous command, "Speak unto the children of Israel, that they go forward."

Subject. The same message is delivered by GOD's priests to you now.

1. To all who have escaped out of Egypt.
2. To all who are in doubt and perplexity.

Point I. *To all who have escaped out of Egypt.*

Egypt is set in Holy Scripture as a type of the bondage of sin. And the leaving Egypt represents the conversion from a state of sin, the leaving the old slavery to passion and vice, an escape from the power of Pharaoh, the hard task-master, Satan.

Now observe, to have escaped, to have broken the chain, deserted the work of Satan, is not enough.

No! there is still something to do; those thus escaped are not safe, because they have cast away their bondage. Satan is sure to pursue them, sure to surround them. If they sit down in complacent satisfaction, and say, 'I am converted, I am now all right and safe, one of the elect, predestined to life!' then, before they are aware, Satan has them again in his power. No! for all who have broken with sin the message comes, "Speak unto the children of Israel, that they go forward." And how?

To what did the Israelites "go forward?" They went forward—

1. To Sinai, the law of the Most High. 2. To the partaking of manna, angels' food. 3. To conflict with their enemies in the wilderness.

To these three things must the converted soul "go forward." It must advance to the law of God, the keeping of the commandments; it must go forward to sacramental partaking of angels' food; it must go forward to struggle and conquest over self-will, the lust of the flesh, the lust of the eye, and the pride of life.

Point II. *To all in perplexity.*

When the way is dark before you, so that you see not your path; when your foes press you on every side, and an impassable barrier seems to be before you; then take a bold and resolute step—*go forward.*

I am girded in with temptation; I cannot serve God as I would desire, the household cares, the weekly business, perplex and harass me! What then can I do?—*Go forward.*

I know not how to overcome those old bad habits which have got such fast hold of me, to break from those companions who lead me away. Never was any one in such a predicament as I am! What shall I do?—*Go forward.*

I know that God would have me love my enemies, meet railing with blessing, and enmity with good will—but I cannot; what, then, can I do?—*Go forward.*

God's presence is hid from me, my prayers are cold, my mind cannot fix itself on God, I am indifferent to religion, discontented with everything around me, despondent about myself. What is to be done?—at once, I say, *Go forward.*

And, lastly, I see death before me, and I shudder on the bank. I recoil before its mysterious terrors!—Boldly, confidently, gladly, *Go forward.*

Point III. *The ways of advance.*

You ask, how go forward? Into what shall I enter?

I cannot answer each soul individually, but I say—Is there a means of grace, a sacrament, any decided step, any great act of self-renunciation, from which you have hitherto shrunk, about which you have hesitated? Then, I say, when perplexity falls on you, difficulties beset you from which it seems impossible for you to disentangle yourself—take that step, frequent that sacrament, use that means of grace.

Conclusion. Lastly, this command is addressed to all. It is the watchword of every Christian; even from Baptism to the end of the warfare, "Go forward!" never relinquish a duty, never retreat before Satan, never yield an inch of ground; to all and every one comes the command,—"Speak unto the children of Israel, that they go forward."

XXI.

THE CROWNS OF JOSHUA.

"*Take silver and gold, and make crowns, and set them upon the head of Joshua, the son of Josedech, the high priest.*"—Zech. vi. 11.

Introduction. Description of the vision. Zechariah makes crowns, one of silver, the other of gold, and places them on the head of Joshua. At the same time he seats him on the throne of dominion, and of the priesthood. Afterwards these crowns are given to Helem, Tobijah, Jediah and Hen, to be kept in the temple, and a prophecy is uttered: "Behold the Man whose name is the Branch; and He shall grow up out of His place, and He shall build the temple of the LORD; even He shall build the temple of the LORD; and He shall bear the glory, and shall sit and rule upon His throne; and He shall be a priest upon His throne; and the counsel of peace shall be between them both. And they that are far off shall come and build in the temple of the LORD, and ye shall know that the LORD of hosts hath sent me unto you." (verses 12—15.)

Subject. *The interpretation of this vision.*

Joshua signifies JESUS—identity of name. For JESUS too crowns are made, one of gold, and one of silver; He is crowned as King and as Priest, He sits and rules as King, and He is "Priest upon His throne" as well. Then He gives these crowns to others as a memorial in the temple for ever; i.e., He communicates His royal and priestly authority to certain men in the temple He had founded, which is His Church.

Point I. *Christ as King.*

Of this David prophesied, "I have set my King upon my holy hill of Zion. I will preach the law, whereof the LORD hath said unto Me, Thou art My SON, this day have I begotten Thee;" also, "Thy throne, O GOD, is for ever and ever, a sceptre of righteousness is the sceptre of Thy Kingdom; Thou hast loved righteousness and hated iniquity, therefore GOD, even Thy GOD, hath anointed Thee with the oil of gladness above Thy fellows."

CHRIST was typified by Melchizedek, King of Salem, and

Priest of the Most High GOD. CHRIST is the Prince of Peace, "and of His Kingdom," we are told, "there shall be no end."

Now CHRIST speaks continually of His Kingdom, the Kingdom of Heaven, and He speaks of it as constituted upon earth, and therefore as having in it imperfections.

A king rules over a kingdom—CHRIST's Kingdom is the Church. Joshua's golden crown was given to men in the temple—so CHRIST gave His authority to certain men He had chosen to rule His Kingdom: "As My FATHER hath sent Me, even so send I you." "He breathed on them and said, Receive ye the HOLY GHOST: go teach all nations." The first generation of these rulers were called Apostles. But this generation was not to pass away; they ordained others to succeed them, conveying to them their authority. The subsequent generations are called bishops. These are they to whom the golden crown of authority in the temple is conveyed. They are the magistrates of CHRIST's Kingdom; ruling during His absence.

Point II. *Christ as Priest.*

"Thou art a Priest for ever, after the order of Melchizedek." "This man hath an unchangeable priesthood," says S. Paul. A priest is one who offers a sacrifice. The sacrifice of CHRIST is Himself.

But the silver crown was also given to men in the temple, and CHRIST ordained men to act as priests in His kingdom, and to offer continually sacrifice before GOD the FATHER; not a different sacrifice, but the same—CHRIST Himself. In the temple were two sacrifices, Incense and Blood. We offer the incense of prayer and praise along with the priest who leads the service; and he offers blood when, in the Eucharist, he pleads before GOD the Sacrifice of CHRIST's death.

Conclusion. "They that are far off," says GOD in this vision, "shall come and build in the temple of the LORD, and ye shall know that the LORD of Hosts hath sent me unto you."

Glorious thought! we in the Catholic Church are builders with Him in the temple; we, though far off, are subjects of this great Kingdom, under the protection of this great King. We, though far off, are made nigh by His Blood, through which we obtain remission of our sins, declared by the priesthood in His temple acting in His name.

XXII.

THE SEVEN-BRANCHED CANDLESTICK.

"*I have looked, and behold a candlestick all of gold, with a bowl upon the top of it, and his seven lamps thereon, and seven pipes to the seven lamps which are upon the top thereof; and two olive trees by it.*"—Zech. iv. 2, 3.

Introduction. Zechariah has been shown the mystery of the rebuilding of the Church, and the consecration of the Christian ministry, under the figure of Joshua, the son of Josedech; and now GOD shows him, in vision, the inner life of the Church, and its spiritual connection with CHRIST.

One vision showed Zechariah the construction of the Church; the next showed him the Royalty and Priesthood therein. This vision shows him the Sacramental System, and its connection with CHRIST.

Signification of the Vision. The golden candlestick is the visible Church (see also Rev. i.) In the Revelation of S. John, the seven churches of Asia are represented as seven golden candlesticks, in the midst of which stands CHRIST. But here, to represent the unity of the Church, it is figured as *one*. So our LORD speaks of His Church as visible and one, "a city that is set on a hill;" that hill or rock is Himself. The candlestick is *golden*, to represent the incorruptibility of its faith, for gold will not rust or tarnish. So the Church, the pillar and ground of the faith, cannot fail to teach the right faith.

The *seven lamps* represent different degrees of the faithful in the Church. Thus CHRIST bids His disciples—"Let your loins be girded about, and your lights burning;" "ye are the light of the world." Of John Baptist it was said, "He was a burning and a shining light;" and CHRIST says of His followers, that they are "children of light."

Then there, are *two olive trees*, or (v. 12) "two olive branches which through the two golden pipes empty the golden oil out of themselves."

Zechariah has already given us the clue to the meaning of this, for he has spoken of CHRIST as the Branch. But here we have the branch made twain. This signifies the two natures of CHRIST, as the one branch signified the unity of His Person.

These two olive branches convey golden oil to the lamps by "seven pipes" (v. 2.) What then are these golden pipes which convey the golden oil from CHRIST to the faithful, and preserve in them the flame of faith?

1. The little child gathers its sweet innocence, its childish faith, its pure simplicity, its love of JESUS, from the golden channel of Baptism.

2. The youth goes forth to fight boldly against the world, the flesh, and the devil, and whence does he gather the strength to wage a victorious warfare, but by the gift of

supernatural power distilled through the golden channel of Confirmation?

3. The penitent who mourns over lost grace, whose past is one of darkness, whose lamp has well-nigh gone out, how can he regain brilliancy, how can his bowl be filled again with cleansing, invigorating oil, save through the golden channel of Penance?

4. And you who strive to live closest to GOD, who desire to have your bodies sanctified by CHRIST's Body, and your souls washed in His most precious Blood, what is the source of your strength, and faith, and hope, and zeal, but the golden oil dropping from the Manhood and Godhead of CHRIST flowing to you through the golden channel of the Eucharist?

5. Again, to those who desire to enter the marriage state, grace is needed, that they may be able to bear with one another, and to love one another in constancy; a new state demands a new overflow of grace, and lo! it gushes responsive to their requirements through the golden channel of Matrimony.

6. So also to those who seek the ministry, special grace is needed, and the golden oil anointing them streams from CHRIST through the golden channel of Holy Order.

7. And lastly, death comes on, and the last struggle with Satan and his host; they make their final and most desperate assault to destroy, when the body and mind are most enfeebled; is there no special outburst of divine grace to strengthen the dying against these special temptations? Surely yes! through the golden channel of Extreme Unction the anointing oil is shed.

Conclusion. But observe, that Zechariah speaks (in verse 12) of "the two golden pipes" that "empty the golden oil out of themselves," distinguishing two of the seven as pre-eminent. These are the two "sacraments of the Gospel" "which are generally necessary to salvation," viz., Baptism and the Holy Eucharist. These are absolutely necessary to all, but the others are only necessary to special conditions of life; necessary to some, but not necessary to all.

And finally, learn—

1. That what we see in the sacraments are the visible, natural channels conveying invisible supernatural grace from CHRIST.

2. Not to despise them because they have a visible, palpable, material exterior, for they are the appointed channels for conveying invisible, impalpable, immaterial grace.

3. Not to expect to keep our lamps burning without using them.

XXIII.

DIFFICULTIES.

"*Who art thou, O great mountain? before Zerubbabel thou shalt become a plain.*"—Zech. iv. 7.

Introduction. Zerubbabel was engaged in rebuilding the temple, but insuperable difficulties, as it seemed to all, arose. No doubt he was discouraged, and began to despair; then came the word of GOD to him—"Who art thou, O great mountain? before Zerubbabel thou shalt become a plain;" in spite of all hindrances put in his way, in spite of every impossibility that now stared him in the face, he would succeed.

Subject. These words of consolation may also be used of the Church and of us.

Point I. *The mountain of difficulties impeding and opposing the Church.*

They are manifest enough. Oh! what a mountain of prejudice against all that gives honour to God! Do the faithful sons of God strive to build up the ruined sanctuary, to restore the waste places, to beautify the temple of the Lord? what a huge mass of prejudice is opposed to them! jealousy of all that honours God, grudging against all that glorifies not man but God.

Oh! what a mountain of unbelief and misbelief rises against the truth! Do we teach the true faith in all its integrity, the Real Presence, the Eucharistic Sacrifice, Penance, Self-denial? the mountain is before us, a cumbrous mass of heresy or doubt.

Oh! what a mountain of abuse stands in the way of the Church displaying her activity to win souls to Christ! This is not lawful, that is illegal, none but the one old rut must be run in that has been cut by Act of Uniformity; the Church lives, and she is treated as though she were a piece of mechanism.

But there is comfort. What art thou, O great mountain of prejudice! oh great mountain of unbelief! oh great mountain of abuse! before Christ, our true Zerubbabel, restoring His Holy Temple, thou shalt become a plain.

Point II. *The mountain of difficulties impeding and opposing the advance of the soul.*

Is there no mountain opposed to you? Your temptations, your difficulties, your associations? You feel a call from God to a special course, but a mountain is before you. You feel a desire to serve God better than heretofore, but a mountain is in the way. Fear not! it is not you, but Christ, that dwelleth in you, who is your might, and before Him the mountain will become a plain. And how, do you ask? hear the words of God.

Conclusion. "Not by might, nor by power, but by My Spirit, saith the Lord of hosts." (verse 6.)

XXIV.

THE OVERTHROW OF GOD'S ENEMIES.

"*Then lifted I up mine eyes, and saw, and behold, four horns. And I said unto the angel that talked with me, What be these? And he answered me, These are the horns which have scattered Judah, Israel, and Jerusalem. And the Lord showed me four carpenters. Then said I, What come these to do? And he spake, saying, These are the horns which have scattered Judah, so that no man did lift up his head: but these are come to fray them, to cast out the horns of the Gentiles, which lifted up their horn over the land of Judah to scatter it.*"—Zech. i. 18—21.

Introduction. Zechariah saw in this vision the powers of the four quarters of the world, symbolized by four horns, dispersing Israel and Judah: that is, on the north, the Syrians and Chaldæans; on the south, the Egyptians and Edomites; on the east, the Moabites and Ammonites; and on the west, the Roman power. And God showed that He had prepared destruction for each of these powers which cruelly entreated His people. Against each, however high it might lift its horn, a carpenter was prepared, who would destroy it; a carpenter, or workman either in wood or iron, for the original word signifies either, who, an emissary of the Most High, would "fray it."

Subject. *So also against every persecutor of the Church a carpenter has made ready his tools.*

Point I. In the original signification of the parable, the workman, or carpenter, signified some poor, insignificant means, employed by GOD to overthrow the world-power which thrust sore at His elect, and scattered them into all lands. And so even now, "GOD has chosen the foolish things of the world to confound the wise; and GOD hath chosen the weak things of the world to confound the things which are mighty; and base things of the world, and things which are despised, hath GOD chosen; yea, and things which are not, to bring to nought things that are." (1 Cor. i. 27, 28.)

We are often much disquieted with the aspect of affairs. The Church seems threatened with dissolution, the faithful are scattered as sheep without a shepherd, the world-power masters the Church and binds her hand and foot with red tape, that she cannot move to perform her work, nor utter her voice to proclaim her authority.

We are often much disquieted with the assaults upon faith. Science seems to corrode the foundations of belief in the supernatural; criticism to destroy the inspiration of Scripture; heresy to snap asunder the authority of the Church.

We are uneasy, the horn is lifted very high, the horn of the world-power, the horn of speculative infidelity, and we feel despair. But never fear. The LORD has prepared a carpenter, and in His own time He will produce him to fray those horns. What the feeble instrument will be we know not; but, though feeble, it will succeed.

Point II. But there is a deep signification in the destroyers of the horns being called carpenters. Does not that point to who is the destroyer of the horns which thrust and scatter the true Israel, the Church of GOD? Is not our Defender, He Who will rescue us, One Who was called "the carpenter's Son," One Whose youth was spent in the carpenter's shop with axe and saw, and chisel and plane?

It is said that Julian the apostate, just before the battle in which he perished, turned to a Christian soldier, and said, with a sneer, "*Well, what is the carpenter's Son about now?*" "Sire," answered the soldier, "*He is making a coffin.*"

See how some great legislator achieves a triumph by passing some bill, or framing some law which will curtail the liberties of the Church, and impede her action, check her life-blood, interfere with her efficiency. In the moment of success, as he finds the faithful afflicted and perplexed—"Ah! what have I done! and what is the carpenter's Son about now?" Poor, wretched man! I will tell you—He is making a coffin for your power.

See how a powerful Council sits, and plots, and plans to insult JESUS, by robbing Him of those external marks of honour which the Church has ordered to be given to Him in token of her love and reverence to Him. Then the Council does the deed of wickedness, and triumphant in its profanity, exclaims, "Ah ha! no more bowed knee, no mark of worship, comely vestment, and lighted taper, and fragrant incense, in honour of the LORD of Glory. Ah ha! carpenter's Son, chips and sawdust alone for Thee, no regal splendour. We have conquered; what is the carpenter's Son about now?" Oh fools! in your madness outraging the King of Heaven! what is the carpenter's Son about? He is making a coffin for your characters.

See how some man of science has hit upon a truth, and that truth he uses as a lever to upset Revelation; and, all exultant at his discovery, he cries, "Ha! no more faith, we walk by sight; away with the supernatural—everything is natural. Ah ha! carpenter's Son, we have shorn Thee of

Thy Divinity, and reduced Thee to Thy proper level—an excellent man, who is dead and buried, and gone to dust eighteen hundred years ago. The carpenter's Son, what is He about now?" Poor fool! another discovery will upset thy demonstration. He is making a coffin for thy science!

Conclusion. And now one word to conclude. In quietness and confidence is our strength. In quietness, because greater is He that is with us than he that is against us. In confidence, because He is the Carpenter able and ready to fray every horn that lifts up itself on high against His people; able and ready to build a coffin for every persecutor of His elect.

XXV.

THE PROVING OF MEN.

"*It shall come to pass, that in all the land, saith the Lord, two parts therein shall be cut off and die; but the third part shall be left therein. And I will bring the third part through the fire, and will refine them as silver is refined, and will try them as gold is tried: they shall call on My Name, and I will hear them: I will say, It is My people: and they shall say, The Lord is my God.*"—Zech. xiii. 8, 9.

Introduction. This prophecy of Zechariah follows a succession of visions in which were revealed to him the building and constitution of the Church. The meaning of this prophecy seems to be that of all the inhabitants of the world, one part will be heathen, one part will be heretical, and one part will belong to the Catholic Church, and profess the orthodox faith, and that this portion will be tried and purified.

Point I. *The prophecy refers to the Church generally.*

Have you ever seen a blacksmith hammering a piece of red-hot iron? Sparks fly off at every blow. The sparks are worthless, but the mass is moulded into the desired shape for the destined purpose.

Now God is just so moulding His Church. "Ye shall be persecuted of all men for My sake." It is good for the Church that so it should be. We must expect the Church to be hit, and hit hard; hit by the state, hit by the newspapers, hit by popular opinion, hit by popular tumults. But the mass is thereby being moulded.

However, during the process sparks fly off, bright and dazzling they are as they dash away, but they fall down dross. Heavy blows are being now dealt the Church in this land by state interference, by iniquitous judgments, by popular clamour. We must expect more blows, and worse ones—let them come. God uses the hammer to make the mass compact. And does not each blow consolidate the mass? Has not each stroke broken down prejudice, and driven together those who were estranged? Has not each shock thrust those of the Low Church who love Jesus nearer to the High Church, and pressed the Anglicans and the Catholics together? And may we not hope that as infidelity and spiritual wickedness in high places deal heavier blows, the severed parts of the Church, the Orientals, the Romans, and ourselves, will be welded together into one compact mass, in which our miserable prejudices will disappear?

But it must not be forgotten that as the work proceeds, the worthless sparks will fly off, and make a great flash in their apostasy.

Point II. *Individual application.*

But you, too, as well as the Church, will be tried and refined. Have you ever seen the rough metal, the mass of spar with a few yellow streaks in it, much spar and little gold? What is done with that? It is crushed and washed in many waters.

Have you ever seen the black stone out of which silver is extracted? What is done with that? It is burned in the fire, and the silver dribbles out.

So must you be tried in the water of purification, in the fire of temptation; that what is worthless may disappear, what is precious may be refined.

You will be tried with temptation, with disappointment, and with weariness in your work.

Conclusion. Remember GOD tries you as (1) members of the Church, and (2) as private individuals; but oh! what comfort, oh! what joy! "They shall call on My Name, and I will hear them: I will say, It is My people; and they shall say, The LORD is my GOD."

XXVI.

THE SIGN TAU.

"*Go through the midst of the city, through the midst of Jerusalem, and set a mark upon the foreheads of the men that sigh and that cry for all the abominations that be done in the midst thereof.*"—Ezek. ix. 4.

Introduction. In the preceding chapter GOD had showed the prophet Ezekiel four great iniquities of the chosen people in the city and temple. He now tells him that He will destroy this rebellious people and save only a remnant.

And this He makes clear to him by a vision. Describe vision.[1]

Interpretation. I. *First fulfilment.*

This vision and prophecy was exactly fulfilled when Jerusalem was given up to slaughter by the Romans. Then men, women, and children were destroyed, and only those signed with the Tau, the cross, escaped; for in the destruction of Jerusalem no Christian perished.

II. *Second fulfilment.*

But there is a further signification. Jerusalem, the chosen city, is the Church, and the history of the chosen city is in a great measure a foreshadowing of the history of the Church. The Church too will be full of abominations of all kinds—idolatry of intellect, idolatry of Royal Supremacy, idolatry of wealth; contempt of sacraments, scorn of priestly authority, disregard of GOD's Word, disbelief in the spiritual world.

Before the end, the Church will be full of wickedness. Nevertheless, a remnant will remain of faithful ones sighing over the desolation.

And the time of the end approaches.

Six angels are sent forth with weapons—are sent forth, as they were sent of old, against the Egyptians and against the Assyrians, with orders to slay.

But the *seventh angel* is different from the six who are armed to slay; He is JESUS CHRIST Himself. His mission is to mark His own. He is represented clothed in the

[1] In the Vulgate, "et signa Thau super frontes virorum gementium." The Tau was the old Hebrew character shaped like a cross. The word for *sign* or mark used by the prophet is תָּו *Tau*, meaning, as Gesenius says in his Lexicon, *signum cruciforme;* and he adds that on the old Hebrew coins the Tau was always made as a cross +.

white linen of the eternal priesthood, and having at his side the *inkhorn*, as the inditer of the New Testament. He goes through the city, and marks with the cross His chosen remnant.

Tau, the cross, is the last letter of the Hebrew alphabet, and signifies completion. The Jews, when they set up CHRIST's Cross on Calvary, marked as it were by that sign the finishing of their day of grace, the completion of their covenant. At the end of the world "the sign of the Son of Man" will appear in the heavens, as token that the New Covenant is closed, that the day of probation for the Church is accomplished.

Conclusion. Now observe who are signed and are saved. It is *they who mourn*—those who see and lament over the iniquity and worldliness in the Church.

Also let us look to ourselves, that the Cross be signed on us, on our brows, on our lips, and on our hands; that in all we think, and say, and do, CHRIST's mark may be manifest, that all may know that we are CHRIST's disciples.

XXVII.

THE CROWN OF LIFE.

"*Henceforth there is laid up for me a crown of righteousness, which the Lord the righteous judge shall give me at that day: and not to me only, but unto all them also that love His appearing.*"—2 Tim. iv. 8.

Introduction. The story is told of a virgin martyr, that at her trial she spoke of the crown of life laid up for her in heaven. A bystander jestingly said, "Promise to let me see that crown." The saint turned and looked at him, and said, "I promise." The night after her passion she appeared to him in a dream, with a crown of dazzling beauty on her head, and another of inferior beauty, but still very glorious, in her hand, which she offered to him. When he woke, he hastened to confess CHRIST, and win the proffered crown by martyrdom.

Subject. 1. *The Crown.* 2. *How preserved, and how lost.*

Point I. The crown was offered to the Jews, (Ezek. xvi. 12,) "I put a jewel on thy forehead—a beautiful crown upon thy head."

GOD addresses the Jewish nation as a woman rescued from want. He says He washed her in pure water, and anointed her with oil, He crowned her, and fed her with honey, and with flour of wheat, and then—she forsook Him and turned to other lovers, and thereupon her crown was cast away, her raiment was stripped off, and—polluted and vile, she was rejected by Him.

(Ezek. xxi. 26,) "O thou profane Israel, whose day is come, when iniquity shall have an end, Thus saith the LORD GOD, Remove the diadem and take off the crown." So too does Jeremiah lament, "The crown is fallen from our head; woe unto us, that we have sinned."

Thus, in a figure, we see the election, the sin, and the rejection of the Jewish nation.

Now this figure applies to us.

The crown is offered, nay it is given to us. We have been washed in pure water at our Baptism; we have been rescued from wretchedness and chosen of GOD; we have been anointed with the unction of the HOLY GHOST in Confirmation; we have been fed with honey and the flour of wheat in the Holy Eucharist. Ours is the crown set with the seven stones, Humility, Liberality, Meekness, Temperance, Brotherly Love, Diligence, and central, over the brow, Purity.

Point II. Such is the crown of righteousness which is ours. How shall we use it? Shall we pluck out the gems and divest it of its chief splendour? By indulging in pride you break out the gem Humility; by avarice, by anger, by intemperance, by envy, you rob your crown of one jewel after another, and last and saddest loss of all, you may lose the virginal star of Purity. That gem can never be replaced. You may supply the empty socket with purple Repentance, but never again with the white diamond of Virginity.

Oh, young people, to you I speak with great earnestness, and give you timely advice.

And you advanced Christians, beware lest you who have been washed in pure water, have been anointed with the HOLY GHOST, have been robed in Christian virtues, that fed on the honey of GOD's word and the flour of wheat in the Holy Eucharist, lest you fall as did the Jews, and lose your crown.

Conclusion. There is comfort and there is caution in the consideration of the crown—caution lest it be lost, or injured, or spoiled of its beauty; comfort in knowing that every repentant tear brightens it, every struggle against sin adds to it a glory.

XXVIII.

TRUE AND FALSE CONVERSION.

"*Beloved, believe not every spirit, but try the spirits whether they are of God: because many false prophets are gone out into the world.*"—1 S. John iv. 1.

Introduction. It has been prophesied that in the latter days men shall heap to themselves teachers, having itching ears, and shall turn away their ears from the truth. Our LORD warns us that there shall be false prophets and false spirits about, and that the devil himself will appear as an angel of light. "Such," says S. Paul, "are false apostles, deceitful workers, transforming themselves into the apostles of CHRIST. And no marvel; for Satan himself is transformed into an angel of light. Therefore it is no great thing if his ministers also be transformed as the ministers of righteousness, whose end shall be according to their works," (2 Cor. xi. 13—15.) Again, (S. Matth. xxiv. 11, 24,) "Many false prophets shall arise and shall deceive many. For there shall arise false Christs and false prophets, and shall show great signs and wonders; insomuch that if it were possible, they shall deceive the very elect. Behold, I have told you."

Point I. If we consider how it is most likely that Satan could injure souls, and deceive the elect, we shall conclude that it would be by some ingenious setting up of a false religion which, with a show of zeal for GOD, should cut away the grounds on which man can alone be saved.

Suppose GOD has ordained that a sinner shall be saved in

this way. First, he must have a consciousness of his sin; then he must repent of his sin and confess it; then he must amend his life; and in order that he may amend his life GOD gives grace or supernatural assistance.

Now this is precisely the way GOD has ordained.

How then could the devil best ruin souls, but by effecting a disbelief in this scheme, and by setting up another in its stead, which would be so plausible as to deceive many, but which would run directly contrary to that ordained by GOD?

Now there is such a scheme drifting about among men. It is this. That the sinner may be saved, he must first be convinced of his sin; then he must feel in himself assurance of pardon; thereupon he is placed in a state of salvation from which he cannot fall away.

This scheme cuts at the root of repentance, and destroys amendment of life, and prevents man from applying for grace, for he feels the battle is over, he is converted, sin has no more dominion over him.

I think it is impossible to doubt that this doctrine of Justification is of Satanic origin. It is that of which the Prophet Jeremiah speaks, (vi. 14—16,) "They have healed the hurt of my people slightly, saying, Peace, peace; when there is no peace. Were they ashamed when they had committed abomination? nay, they were not at all ashamed, neither could they blush: therefore they shall fall among them that fall: at the time that I visit them they shall be cast down, saith the LORD. Thus saith the LORD, Stand ye in the ways and see, and ask for the old paths, where is the good way, and walk therein, and ye shall find rest for your souls. But they said, We will not walk therein."

Point II. True conversion is something very different from that described. Examples of SS. Peter, Paul, Mary

Magdalene. Its fruits are humility, meekness, modesty, self-government, confusion of face, and amendment of life.

True conversion consists in deep repentance for sin, and a life-long struggle against temptation; it is accompanied by a spirit of fear. "Go, sin no more, lest a worse thing come upon thee," is a text ever present to the truly converted.

Conclusion. Therefore shun noisy, deceptive scenes of conversion; for these conversions are prophesied of as false. They are contrary to CHRIST's scheme of redemption. Rather, in the words of Jeremiah, ask for the old Church paths of penance, and walk therein, "and ye shall find rest for your souls."

XXIX.

JUSTIFICATION BY FAITH.

"*Ye see how that by works a man is justified, and not by faith only.*"—S. James ii. 24.

Introduction. There are few doctrines more misconceived than that of Justification by Faith. Of Justification by Faith, S. Paul speaks much,—he opposes it to the works of the Law; but then he gives to Justification by Faith a meaning totally distinct from that given to it now-a-days. The modern doctrine was invented three hundred years ago by one Martin Luther, and it had never been heard of in the Church before, by S. Paul or any one else; but instead of giving it a newly-invented name, he gave it a name of something entirely different, which did exist. We talk of a musket now as a firearm; of old, before the invention of guns, it meant a sparrowhawk; we speak in praise of humility now, but in heathen days the word meant mean and sneaking. So Luther gave an old name to a new patent, and tried thereby to pass it off as an antique.

Point I. *Meaning of Justification by Faith.*

This is what S. Paul meant by Justification by Faith. Justification means the making just in the sight of GOD; the removal of what offends GOD, and the acquisition of that which is well pleasing to GOD. This is precisely what the Jewish system was unable to effect; the Jewish sacraments could neither remove evil nor implant grace.

By Faith S. Paul means that system of communicating invisible grace ordained by CHRIST, which can only be seen by faith, but which is hidden to the eye of flesh.

In the Jewish rites the eye of flesh saw all that there really was in the sacrifice, or the water, or the ashes used in purifications. In the Christian rites the eye of Faith pierces the veil, and sees Divine Grace operating through the visible envelope.

Justification by Faith, according to its Scriptural signification, therefore, means the reconciliation of man to GOD by means of that system which demands the presence of Faith to perceive its significance, i.e., the Sacramental system.

Point II. *Popular misconception.*

The popular idea of the doctrine is, however, widely different.

This is the Lutheran notion, that the whole work of our Justification is wrought by GOD and accepted by us through Faith—that our own efforts and the sacraments are of no avail. All our efforts are no use, as Justification is a free gift of GOD, and sacraments are without profit, as we, having no conflict to fight, nothing to do, need no grace to strengthen us to fight, and enable us to do.

The result of this heresy is—

1. Neglect of Sacraments.
2. Disregard of Repentance.
3. General Demoralization.

Conclusion. The Sacramental system explained as the union of Christ the God-Man with us men to strengthen and enable us by supernatural power conveyed to us through visible channels.

XXX.

ON MERIT.

"*Remember me, O my God, concerning this, and wipe not out my good deeds that I have done for the house of my God, and for the offices thereof.*" —Neh. xiii. 14.

Introduction. Zeuxis the painter was reproached by Agatharchus for the slowness with which he painted. Zeuxis answered, "I paint for eternity." So should all our works be done. How wonderful is the prayer of Nehemiah, when he had completed his work. He had cleansed the chambers of the Temple, and had "brought thither again the vessels of the house of God, with the meat-offerings and the frankincense." He restored among the Jews, after the captivity, the custom of giving tithes to the Levites, and then he exclaims to God, "Remember me, O my God, concerning this, and wipe not out my good deeds that I have done for the house of my God."

He had done more—he obliged the Jews to observe the Sabbath and renounce their profanation of it. And then he exclaims to God, "Remember me, O my God, concerning this also, and spare me according to the greatness of Thy mercy."

Ask a Protestant whether one might desire God to remember one's deeds—such as restoring a Church, teaching the ignorant and the like,—for good, and he will reply that such a prayer is presumption and blasphemy; nevertheless it is Scriptural, as you see.

Moreover, we read in the Acts that an angel was sent to Cornelius to bring him to baptism and the truth, because his alms and prayers had "come up for a memorial before God," (Acts x. 4.)

Subject. Certain works then are meritorious, and deserve God's favour. What then must be their marks?

1. *They must be done according to God's will.*

Abbot Ammon said to a young hermit who sought his advice, "In whatever you do, inquire what is the will of God."

So the Apostle, "Prove what is that good and acceptable and perfect will of God." So Christ our exemplar, "I do always those things that please Him."

2. *They must be done with a right intention.*

That is to say, they must be done, not out of natural good-nature, or from an inferior or wrong motive, but they must spring out of a principle. For instance, there is no merit in giving to a beggar to be relieved of his importunity; there is no merit in subscribing handsomely to a charity because it is expected of you to give a certain sum, and you will be thought shabby if you give less; there is no merit in building a Church or a hospital, or doing any other sumptuous act of munificence, as a bid for votes for the next election, or to get yourself a name. Or again, going to Church, because it is the custom, abstaining from intemperance because it injures health, being respectable because it pays.

No, there must be a right motive, a Christian principle, as the root and spring of the action, or it is worthless.

3. *They must be done out of love or fear of God.*

You see I mention two motives or governing principles—Fear and Love. Of these fear is a very inferior motive. If we abstain from sin because we dread hell, it is a much lower principle to act upon than if we abstain because we love God; just as in a child, you prefer to see it obey its parents because it loves them and is pained to offend them, rather than because it dreads punishment, if it transgresses their orders.

Indeed, a work done out of fear is scarcely to be regarded as meritorious—it is passable, but not worthy.

"Let every sacrifice be salted with salt;" as bread made of dough without salt in it is insipid, so are good works without love.

4. *They must be done diligently.*

The good work done out of love is almost sure to be done diligently; but sometimes for a while the heart is less warm, and a chill comes on the affections. Let not then the work be given up. By continuing it diligently the feeble flame is quickened, and the time of coldness is abbreviated. There is "a reward," says S. Paul, "of them that diligently seek" Christ, (Heb. xi. 6.) "Whatsoever ye do, do it heartily, as to the Lord, and not unto men," (Col. iii. 23.) And S. Paul requires that only such a widow shall be taken into the number of religious, "if she have diligently followed every good work," (1 Tim. v. 10.)

5. *They must be done as in God's sight.*

Knowing that His eyes are over the righteous, that He

reads our most secret thoughts, our motives, and the depth of our earnestness.

Conclusion. And finally, let it never be forgotten that no work can be done that deserves a reward, which is not done by the grace of GOD working in us, which grace we receive through His sacraments.

XXXI.

SMALL BEGINNINGS.

"*First the blade, then the ear, after that, the full corn in the ear.*"—S. Mark iv. 28.

Introduction. *When God works, it is from small beginnings*, when He blesses increase, it is increase from little. Throughout His dealings with the world and men this holds true; it is true also in the sphere of religion.

The one couple in Eden became the progenitors of the human race.

The one family of Abraham multiplied, till it became as the stars for number. The little handful in the Upper Chamber became the origin of the holy Church throughout the world.

The mustard-seed becomes a great tree, so that the birds lodge in its branches. The brook becomes a river, and the river becomes a sea.

The little cloud as a man's hand spreads, till the heaven is dark with wind and rain. The seven loaves feed four thousand, and the five loaves five thousand, and the one Body of CHRIST is the food and sustenance of countless souls through many years.

Point I. *The same law holds good in spiritual matters.*

In every soul at Baptism is sown the seed of spiritual life, a tiny feeble germ of life and energy, powerful however to spring up, and spread, and thrust heavenward, and flower, and seed, and ripen, if watered with the early and latter rain of heavenly grace, and warmed by the sunshine of GOD's presence.

Little germs, hardly perceptible at first, and very feeble when showing, which cannot bear the rude blast, or the heedless foot, or the parching frost.

Little germs, which if carefully protected and trained, will grow up into a crop of fragrant, varied, and goodly graces, rejoicing the eyes of angels and pleasant in the sight of men.

Point II. *The same law holds good in all Christian undertakings.*

Every effort for GOD, however small, is not too small to be blessed with increase. Be fruitful and multiply and replenish the earth, is the blessing on all Christian works.

Every struggle with a besetting sin is not sterile; every endeavour after holiness is not alone; every attempt to advance His kingdom is blessed to grow.

Good works never die. However obscure the spot, however lowly the breast in which GOD plants the desire of serving Him, it is blessed. Despise not its smallness—it will "spring and grow man knoweth not how."

Illustration.—Some few monks came into Brittany in ages past, when that country was heathen. They built a rude shed, in which to dwell, and a chapel of moor stones, and then prepared to till the soil. But alas! they had no wheat. Then one spied a robin redbreast sitting on a cross they had set up, and from his beak dangled an ear of wheat.

They drove the bird away, and secured the grain, sowed it, and next year had more; sowed again, and so by degrees were able to sow large fields and gather abundant harvests. If you go now into Brittany and wonder at the waving fields of golden grain, the peasants will tell you all came from Robin Redbreast's ear of corn. And they have turned the redbreast's ear of corn into a proverb.

A young couple begin to lay by, and people smile at their poor economies, but say the old Bretons, "It is Robin Redbreast's ear of corn."

A child begins to show early signs of piety and self-control, and some scoff. "Mock not," say others, "it is Robin Redbreast's ear of corn."

A drunkard breaks off his bad habit. "It will not last," say some. "God prospering him, it may," say others; "remember Robin Redbreast's ear of corn."

A selfish person shows symptoms of charity; "It is Robin Redbreast's ear of corn."

A grievous sinner sheds his first tear. "Oh! despise not that little bitter drop, it may swell into a repentant stream; God may prosper it as He prospered Robin Redbreast's ear of corn."

Conclusion. And I say to you, in whatever state you are, make a beginning of good. Ask God's blessing upon it, and there will spring up, watered from heaven, illumined from above, cherished by the breath of God,—"First the blade, then the ear, after that the full corn in the ear."

XXXII.

THE EUCHARIST A MYSTERY.

"*Verily, Thou art a God that hidest Thyself, O God of Israel, the Saviour.*"—Isa. xlv. 15.

Introduction. After the Last Supper, CHRIST instituted the Blessed Sacrament. Knowing that His hour was come, for "the Sun knoweth his going down," knowing that Satan was desiring to sift His disciples as wheat, He instituted this august mystery to be their strength and solace.

Subject. *The Eucharist a hidden Mystery.*

Point I. When Samson went down to take to himself a wife of the daughters of the Philistines, he found a lion and slew him. Afterwards he found in the carcase a honey-comb; of this he made a riddle, "Out of the eater came forth meat, and from the strong came forth sweetness."

This may be applied to CHRIST. He is the Lion of the tribe of Judah dying, and from Him the eater at the Last Supper came forth the Bread of Life; and from Him the Strongest One, about to spoil Satan the strong one, and take from him his armour wherein he trusted, comes forth the sweetness of the Eucharist.

Who can understand how the Giver can be the Thing given—the strong be also the sweet?

Verily Thou art a GOD that hidest Thyself. The Holy Eucharist is our riddle, a riddle none can interpret but those who have tasted of the sweetness, received the gift, and have had the explanation of the riddle made known to them by CHRIST Himself.

It is a mystery hidden from the wise and prudent, but revealed to babes. It is a mystery which the reason cannot fathom, but which is comprehended at once by faith.

Point II. It is GOD's way to veil Himself, that the bold eye may not discern Him; and only the faithful heart may discern His Presence.

When speaking to Moses He hid Himself in the bush or in the cloud and thick darkness.

To Elijah He appeared as a still small voice.

When He came on earth, He hid Himself in the form of a poor carpenter lad.

When He went up into heaven, He veiled Himself in a cloud.

And now, when He presents Himself before us, it is hidden under Eucharistic symbols.

Point III. But how are you to know Him, to see through His veil?

By faith alone. By faith the shepherds saw in the babe wrapped in swaddling clothes their Messiah. By faith the Magi knew Him Who was laid at a mother's breast to be their LORD and King. By faith S. Peter confessed CHRIST, the poor Rabbi, to be his LORD and his GOD. By faith the thief knew the malefactor hanging on the Cross to be his SAVIOUR having the keys of death and of hell.

But there are many changes in nature to help you to understand the mystery of the transformation in the Eucharist. The rain falls on the roots of the vine and is transformed into sap, and the sap is transformed into wine. You eat bread, and that bread is changed in its substance, so that the substance of the bread becomes the substance of your flesh. You cast a black piece of rock into your grate, and it is changed into warmth-giving fire.

Conclusion. From His altar Christ speaks to us and says, "Lo, as I promised, I have come to you, that you might not be comfortless; but I have come, not in My majesty to dazzle your eyes, but in lowliness and weakness to try your faith, and to test your piety. I have hidden Myself, but come, dear sons of men, pierce the mystery, and with the eye of faith behold Me in My beauty and in My power."

XXXIII.

THE CAKE OF BARLEY.

"*Lo, a cake of barley bread tumbled into the host of Midian, and came unto a tent, and smote it that it fell, and overturned it, that the tent lay along.*"—Judges vii. 13.

Introduction. Narration of the circumstances accompanying this dream.

Signification I. *Gideon*, (chap. vi. 15,) "O my Lord, wherewith shall I save Israel? behold my family is poor in Manasseh, and I am least in my father's house. And the Lord said unto him, Surely I will be with thee."

Signification II. *Christ:* "Whence knoweth this man letters?" "Is not this the carpenter's son?" Was not His family poor in Israel, and He made least in His Father's house, "made a little lower than the angels?"

Yes, Christ is meant by this barley bread—*barley*, because poor, and common, and despised, *bread*, because He said, "I am the Bread of Life." He fell into the host of Satan and smote his power, and cast it down, so that his power lay prostrate.

Signification III. *The Eucharist.* But there is a further meaning in this dream. It is true that, in the first place, it referred to Gideon; it is more true that it refers to CHRIST; it is most true as it speaks of CHRIST in His Sacramental Presence.

How does He appear amongst us now? Is it not in a poor mean symbol? is not the natural outward appearance nothing, and yet, inasmuch as the LORD is present as its substance, mighty?

Has not CHRIST said, "I am the Bread that came down from heaven," "I am the Bread of Life," when speaking of this most august and venerable Sacrament?

Well, and is not the Eucharist mighty? Mighty! it is as mighty as GOD Himself, for it is GOD Himself present in the midst of us.

See how doubt and disbelief arise, and camp against the Church of CHRIST; wide-spread is infidelity, lifted up with pride, thinking to destroy the Faith with its arguments, its bold speculation, its gross materialism; and there, into the midst of the host, falls the cake of barley bread. Some poor feeble maid-servant, some little child, some old labouring man, knows and believes in the miraculous Presence in the Eucharist, and before the simple faith in the Real Presence the tent of infidelity falls and lies along.

See how as of old, in Arian times, so now heresy spreads and poisons the faith of even the bishops and rulers of the Church in England, so that they are with Midian, instead of fighting the LORD's battles; see how the state councils attack the truth, insult and deny the Eucharistic Presence; but the cake of barley bread is stronger than kings, and councils, and apostate prelates, and their tent of an establishment void of dogma is smitten so that it falls, and is overturned, and lies along.

See how the power and cruelty of persecuting tyrants has been exerted against the weak and feeble; children and women have resisted all their might and wicked invention; how so? through their own might? Oh, no. The cake of barley bread was with them, and smote the tent that it fell.

See how Satan encamps with all his temptations against some poor timid soul—tries it with passion, assails it with lust, with doubt, with despondency, uses, in one word, every art to ruin it, but fails utterly. The soul remains unscarred and safe. How is this? Oh! the cake of barley bread is mightier than all the host of Midian.

Conclusion. Here then, my brethren, is your strength—here is that which will fight for you; though a host of men were laid against me, yet will not I fear, the LORD of Hosts is with me in His august and adorable Sacrament.

XXXIV.

EMMANUEL.

"*There standeth one among you, whom ye know not.*"—S. John i. 26.

Introduction. The Incarnation is the descent of GOD to the level of man's necessities. CHRIST is GOD and He is Man; the Infinite and the finite in one, the Spiritual and the material in one, the Supernatural and the natural in one.

Point I. The Law of the Incarnation is the indissoluble union of the spiritual with the material, of the supernatural with the natural. This is applied in several ways.

1. *Divine authority* comes to us through the agency of

men. The Church is the extension of the Incarnation in its authoritative aspect; the Church is spiritual and material, supernatural and natural, divine and human. The material, natural, and human element is the vehicle for conveying the spiritual, supernatural, divine authority to men.

2. *Divine grace* comes to us through outward and visible envelopes. The Sacramental system is the extension of the Incarnation in its grace-giving aspect. The Sacraments are spiritual and material, supernatural and natural at the same time, the two elements are indissolubly united, as the Manhood and Godhead, incapable of separation, in CHRIST.

Point II. It was not enough for the Apostles to go and teach all nations about a CHRIST Who had lived on earth, but was gone beyond sight; no, that was not the glad tidings. The Gospel is the good news of a present CHRIST always in the world as the source of authority, the giver of grace, and the object of worship. It was not only to preach of something that had been, that the Apostles went forth; they went and taught of something that then was—not merely that CHRIST had been on earth some years before, but that He then was on earth in the midst of His Church, Emmanuel, GOD with us.

If CHRIST'S Presence had been given only to a few thousand Jews eighteen hundred years ago, is humanity satisfied thereby? No; the human heart cries out not merely for an historical CHRIST, but for a CHRIST immanent and ever present.

There must then be some extension of the Incarnation to satisfy this requirement.

The Presence was indeed perpetuated. How? In the Eucharist.

Point III. The Incarnation was a manifestation of

CHRIST'S love to us. How are we to be restored to union with Him? By love to Him. Then He must come to receive our love. He does so in the Eucharist. The Eucharist is JESUS stepping forth towards us, and saying, "My son, I love thee, I have descended even to this for thee, that thou, having My Presence on My altars, mayest surround It with love, and offer It your adoration."

Whence sprang the love of the martyr? From the blood of the Lamb ever rilling from the altars of the Catacombs.

Whence springs the zeal of those who go forth to bear the Gospel to the heathen, and conquer the kingdoms to CHRIST? From the altar which keeps alive and burning the flame of charity in their souls, and consumes all self-love.

Whence springs the devotion of the sister of mercy, who labours among the sick of our hospitals? From the altar too.

How is it that in our own land the love of GOD has been iced over? that for three hundred years zeal, charity, and faith have all but disappeared from amongst us? Because the Sacramental Presence has been scarce.

Conclusion. If your hearts are cold, why is it? Because there standeth one among you, and ye know Him not. Oh, the blessedness of believing in the Real Presence of JESUS on our altars. Oh, the happiness of realising that He is there as truly as He was in the manger of Bethlehem, and the workshop of Nazareth, and on the Cross of Calvary. Oh, the consolation of seeing JESUS evidently set forth crucified before us in the Holy Sacrifice. Love kindles like a fire, and we forget ourselves in our devotion to Him.

XXXV.

THE ATTRACTION OF THE EUCHARISTIC PRESENCE.

"*And I, if I be lifted up from the earth, will draw all men unto Me.*"—S. John xii. 32.

Introduction. When King Louis, the Saint, of France, was taken prisoner, the Sultan asked a Host as hostage for the army and King, because he observed the love of Christians toward It, that where the Blessed Sacrament was lights and flowers were lavished, gold and velvets and silks and gems were offered, and worshippers were never wanting.

Subject. *It is a fact that the Holy Eucharist exerts a wondrous attraction upon hearts.*

Point I. How wondrous this is! and it is a matter often noticed, that in continental churches there are always worshippers; that, on the other hand, we may leave our own church doors open from morning till night, and none visit them, except there be service going on, or for the sake of curiosity.

Why is this? Because in the continental churches is the Presence, and in ours it is not. In them the Holy Eucharist is reserved. People know and feel that JESUS is there, and they flock to Him, to fall down before Him, and give Him worship. With us, alas! it is only during the hour of Mass that the Presence is vouchsafed to us; and yet, just think—is not that a great privilege, something that prophets and kings would have longed to have, but which was denied them? For an hour, every morning, JESUS visits our churches, stands in the midst of us, says, Peace be unto you, and shows us His hands and His side.

Oh! what a boon to be with JESUS, with Faith's eye to see Him, to be close to Him, to hold His feet and stay Him till He blesses us.

I once was conversing with a lady, and she said to me,—"Oh! if I had only lived in the time when JESUS CHRIST was on earth, I would have sold my house, and gone to Palestine, that I might see Him and worship Him."

"Madam," said I, "no need for you to visit Palestine; no need for you to wish you had lived eighteen hundred years ago; JESUS CHRIST has come to M——; He was here this morning at half-past seven, on the altar of the Church, and why were you not there to see and worship Him?"

Point II. Love, love, is what we need to take us out of ourselves, and to bring us to the feet of JESUS. "If I be lifted up from the earth, I will draw all men unto Me," He said. And He does draw. The powerful attraction is at work; sick and weary of the icy darkness of the Real Absence proclaimed by heresy, men turn to the light, turn to One who is present, present on every altar where the consecrating words are said. He draws them with the cords of a man; they see Him lifted up, as when Mary raised Him for the adoration of the Magi, and they fall down and worship. Their eyes are opened. No need to preach to them of the Real Presence, they *know* it, as they know that the sun shines, and that there is a GOD who made them. No need to argue with them—it is more than faith that they possess, it is knowledge.

Conclusion. Does JESUS not draw you? Is it not that you are too fully occupied with yourself, that your heart is so engrossed with self that there is no room for Him, that the bands that tie you down are so strong that His powerful attraction cannot snap them? Oh! then make some effort to conquer self; and never, never speak in doubt or disbelief against His Presence, lest He say of you, "All day long have I stretched forth My hands," in vain, "to a perverse and gainsaying people."

XXXVI.

GOD'S AND MAN'S JUDGMENTS.

"*Look not on his countenance, or on the height of his stature: because I have refused him: for the Lord seeth not as man seeth; for man looketh on the outward appearance, but the Lord looketh on the heart.*"—1 Sam. xvi. 7.

Introduction. Description of the circumstances. Eliab, Abinadab, Shammah, and the other sons of Jesse, pass before Samuel, and he thinks of one and then of another, that this must be the man most suitable to be king. But God selects the very one made of least account among the brethren, because He looketh on the heart, and not on the outward appearance.

Subject. *The great difference between the judgments of man and the judgments of God.*

Point I. Let us take a few instances in which this appears very strikingly.

People saw the magnificent Dives, and highly esteemed him, but turned in loathing from the diseased and necessitous Lazarus.

The disciples saw the rich men casting, of their abundance, large gifts into the treasury, and despised the mite of the poor widow.

Adam and Eve had a son, and they highly esteemed him, and called him Cain (possession), for in him they thought they had gotten a great possession; and they had another, whom they so lightly esteemed that they named him Abel (vanity). But which did the LORD GOD esteem?

How highly esteemed was the Pharisee standing at the corner of the street, but there was a little child (S. Timothy) whom CHRIST set in the midst of His disciples, greater than the Pharisee.

Point II. GOD considers the intention of the heart, men the appearance. This is no excuse for us, in almsgiving, to give little and think we do it with a good intention. If there is true love we will give liberally, and not grudge. It is love that GOD looks for. Prayers may be long, fasting may be rigorous, alms may be abundant, but if all this be for display, or for any other motive than love, it is worthless.

"Though I speak with the tongues of men and of angels, and have not charity, I am become as sounding brass or a tinkling cymbal. And though I have the gift of prophecy, and understand all mysteries, and all knowledge; and though I have all faith, so that I could remove mountains, and have not charity, I am nothing. And though I bestow all my goods to feed the poor, and though I give my body to be burned, and have not charity, it profiteth me nothing." (1 Cor. xiii. 1—3.)

Two women quarrelled about a bobbin of wool. Each claimed it. Then the case was brought before a judge. He asked each about what coloured spindle was it wound? One said the spindle was white, the other that it was black.

At the last day our works will be unwound. Oh! this

great act of charity, this excellent work! It is unwound, and behind, in the middle, is found the black spindle of vanity.

Conclusion. Therefore we have two lessons to learn—

1. To prove well our motives prompting us to good.

2. "Judge nothing before the time until the Lord come, who both will bring to light the hidden things of darkness, and will make manifest the counsels of the hearts." (1 Cor. iv. 5.)

XXXVII.

LOOKING TO THE END.

"*He that now goeth on his way weeping, and beareth forth good seed, shall doubtless come again with joy, and bring his sheaves with him.*"—Ps. cxxvi. 7.

Introduction. Description of Egyptian sowing on the overflowed waters of the Nile. "Cast thy bread upon the waters: for thou shalt find it after many days."

Subject. *Sow in hope, looking with confidence to the future.*

Point I. How thoroughly is a farmer's work one of hope! A tradesman expects an immediate return—not so a farmer, his prospects are future; he has to lay out capital and time, and wait in patience; he dresses, and cleanses, and sows, and then looks forward.

In like manner must we sow for eternity; sow looking for the future harvest at the end of the world.

Point II. What are we to sow? I may rather ask, what are we not to sow? Whatsoever God has given us we can sow. Has He given us talents, intellectual faculties, health, bodily activity, wealth, position, influence? Sow them for eternity, sow them for the harvest in confidence, in faith, and in hope.

Any act of self-denial, any suffering borne patiently, any work of love shown to CHRIST or His poor, any effort to produce peace, all these are seed which will spring up and bear fruit at the end of the world.

Conclusion. One must go *weeping* and bearing *good* seed. So only can one return with joy with good measure, pressed down and running over, bearing the sheaves of GOD'S abundant reward to Zion.

XXXVIII.

THE WORLD'S BONDAGE.

"*The Philistines took him, and put out his eyes, and brought him down to Gaza, and bound him with fetters of brass; and he did grind in the prison house.*"—Judges xvi. 21.

Introduction. Samson, the favoured of GOD, the liberator of the people of GOD, what becomes of him when he has fallen under the power of evil? He is turned into a slave, and degraded to the condition of a beast.

Subject. *We have in this a type of the world's bondage.*

Point I. We have other scriptural instances of similar falls:—

The prodigal son sent by the citizen of the far country to keep swine.

Solomon, the wise king, swayed by his idolatrous wives.

The Israelites in Egypt, once the favoured and honoured, then the despised and ill-treated.

The Israelites, once lords of the Promised Land, triumphant everywhere, then fallen under the power of the Philistines, deprived of every weapon, and obliged to go down to the Philistines to sharpen their plough-coulters.

Point II. What was the treatment to which Samson was subjected by the Philistines?

1. *They put out his eyes.* This is one of the first effects of sin. It blinds the eyes to the things that belong to the peace of the soul, it darkens them that they cannot see the *truth*, and thus the soul falls under the power of heresy; and that they cannot see what is *right*, and thus the soul falls under the power of demoralization.

Illustration. The Jew at the time of CHRIST'S coming. There, before him was his Messiah, his Redeemer, his SAVIOUR, but his eyes were holden; he said he saw, therefore his sin remained; he was blind to the truth of the Incarnation and to the morality of CHRIST'S teaching, because he was in sin; and so "now are they hid from thine eyes," said CHRIST.

2. *They brought him down to Gaza.* From the tabernacle, and from the service of GOD, he was removed and taken down to the city of idolatry. And this is what sin effects. It draws away the heart from the worship and service of GOD, and it brings it down to the worship and service of self, pleasure, wealth, and the like. The service of GOD becomes distasteful. No string vibrates in the heart responsive to the note of penitence or of triumph, sounded in the Temple. The silver trumpet is blown, but no echo is given back; the sin-enslaved heart turns from the worship of CHRIST, saying, "It is a weariness, our soul loatheth this light food," and goeth down to Gaza.

To such a soul what are Advent and Christmas, Lent and Easter; what the spread altar, the bell for evensong? Our soul loatheth this light food, give us the pipe and quart-pot in the ale-house instead.

3. *They bound him with brazen fetters.* That comes next. First, the sight is darkened that it cannot see the way of peace, then man deserts that road, and goes down to the idolatry of Gaza; then he is bound there with the habits of sin. Terrible bonds are these, little threads at first, so light that we think they may be easily snapped; but they become more numerous and more strong, till habit of sin becomes a fetter of brass which it is almost impossible to snap and escape from.

4. *They made him grind in the prison.* That comes last. The first charm of sin, the novelty of Gaza, is worn off; the brass fetters have ceased to amuse as gay toys. Then comes the grinding, grinding, grinding in the heavy chains, the round of old sins, no longer giving pleasure, the labour, but without satisfaction; the horrible consciousness that sin is a slavery, from which the will cannot muster courage to escape.

Conclusion. But CHRIST'S "service is perfect freedom." "Take My yoke upon you, and learn of Me, for I am meek and lowly of heart, and ye shall find rest for your souls."

XXXIX.

THE ASSAULTS OF SATAN.

"*And David waxed faint. And Ishbi-benob, which was of the sons of the giant, being girded with a new sword, thought to have slain David.*" —2 Sam. xxi. 15, 16.

Introduction. A description of the incident.

Subject. *A type of Satan's attempts against man.*

Point I. *David waxed faint.* Christians often wax faint in the great warfare of life; they have had a hard struggle, they have overcome many times, and they have been inspired with enthusiasm. Then comes the reaction. They begin to weary of this continued struggle, to rest from it awhile, to yield a little, for the sake of a little quiet, and to wax faint in zeal and enthusiasm. This is sure to come on you. Every one who is in earnest feels this exhaustion and waxes faint. Then, remember, is Satan's opportunity. His assaults when you were in the fervour of your zeal were feints, the real attack is made now.

Point II. *Ishbi-benob took a new sword.* Do you notice this? Is not Satan always trying some new device? May be, he has assailed you with anger, with envy, with selfishness, with despondency, and has failed. Then he waits till you wax faint, and quickly straps on the sword of spiritual pride, and attacks and wounds you.

Illustrations. CHRIST's temptation: Satan tried one new sword after another, as each failed.

David's temptation: when least expecting it, on the top of his house the sword of lust smote him and wounded him to the quick.

Conclusion. Need of vigilance. Certainty of victory not always by violent fighting, but by offering a passive resistance without dealing a blow, by simply opposing the shield of Faith, and resting till the faintness is passed; then it will be found that against the old shield the new sword has been blunted or broken.

XL.

WHEN TO RESIST THE DEVIL.

"*And Benaiah, the son of Jehoiada . . . . slew a lion in a pit in time of snow.*"—2 Sam. xxiii. 20.

Introduction. The sacred chronicler is giving a list of David's valiant men, of their heroic acts and their great encounters.

Among the three mighty men of David was Benaiah; and of him is related the incident chosen for my text.

In these words there are three things to note: 1. What it was he slew. 2. Where he slew it. 3. When he slew it.

Subject. I need hardly point out to you that in this is contained an important lesson.

Point I. *Benaiah slew a lion;* a type this of Satan. "Be sober, be vigilant, because your adversary, the devil, as a roaring lion walketh about, seeking whom he may devour, whom resist, steadfast in the faith." (1 S. Pet. v. 8, 9.)

Point II. *The lion was where least expected,* in a pit, or as it would be better translated, in a cistern. In fact it was in one of those cisterns of water near Jerusalem to which people had common resort. There was always, as may be seen to this day, a stream of people going with their pitchers to these cisterns to fill them for what is requisite in the house. Consequently they are some of the most frequented places there can be in the East, and therefore the last place in the world where you would expect to meet a lion.

Now this is precisely like the artifice of Satan. He endeavours to catch us off our guard, by tempting us just where we least expect temptation. In some places we know there is danger; we fear to be assailed, and there we are on our guard; but it is by laying wait for us when we know there is no danger, and have no fear of an assault, that he hopes to overcome us.

Examples. Nebuchadnezzar, whilst walking on his terrace, enjoying the evening air, and the beauty of his gardens. What possible harm could befall him there? yet it was there that he fell.

Belshazzar at his banquet. What danger could come to him when seated feasting with his great nobles? Yet there the king committed the sin which cost him his kingdom.

Judas amongst the apostles. Where could Judas be safer than amidst the chosen followers of CHRIST, close to the side of GOD, listening to His words, beholding His acts, protected by His power. Yet there he fell.

Point III. *The lion was met when least expected*, in time of snow. The lion lurks in his den in winter, and does not stray over the country. Summer is the time when he is met, not when the winter snows have fallen.

So also Satan assails us when we least expect him; not in times of religious enthusiasm, in the summer of zeal, but when we have cooled down and become indifferent, and the snow has fallen on our hearts; when the shield of Faith is laid down, the sword of the Spirit is put away, when we are least prepared for an assault.

Examples. Moses was performing a miracle with the power of the Almighty, giving drink out of the rock to the thirsty Israelites: surely then, when being used as GOD's instrument, he must have felt secure—but then he committed the sin which excluded him from the land of promise.

Jonah was the mouthpiece of GOD, sent by GOD to preach

to the Ninevites: surely then he must have felt secure? Yes! he felt too secure—for then it was that he sinned.

Cain was offering a sacrifice: surely when engaged in an act of worship, when standing before the altar and making supplication to GOD, he was safe? No! just then envy possessed him, and he went on to murder.

Conclusion. Therefore S. Peter gives us the wholesome advice, "Be sober, be vigilant." Be sober—not carried away with the impetuosity of your feelings at one moment, and cold and indifferent at another; and be vigilant, for at such place and at such time as you least expect, you will meet the lion face to face.

XLI.

THE END OF OUR TOIL.

"*I cast the gold into the fire, and there came out this calf.*"—Exod. xxii. 24.

Introduction. A description of the circumstances of the making of the golden calf. Then a description of the erection and adornment of the tabernacle, with the offerings of the people.

Subject. The same contrast continues. The temple of the living GOD, and the idol still demand of us, and still to them do we pour out, our gold.

Point I. *Gold given to the calf.*

What is this gold that we give? Our faculties and our time. Story of Cardinal Wolsey:—Had I but served my GOD with half the zeal I served my king, He would not in mine age have left me naked to mine enemies." (Henry VIII. act iii. sc. 2.) Our energies: "He that soweth to the flesh shall of the flesh reap corruption." (Gal. vi. 8.)

Our hearts and their affections.

Imagine a risen man at the last day reviewing his work: Oh! all that time which was given me, all those talents I possessed, all that natural good that was in me, all my health, my means, my opportunities, my thoughts, my affections cast into the fire—and there came out this calf! I cast everything into the fire of the world's struggle, I suffered, I bore labour, I underwent humiliation, I denied myself pleasure, I wanted to make myself a place, a name, a fortune—and there came out this calf?

"What has it all resulted in? Where is there anything remaining of that which I strove for and acquired? Where is the fruit of those years of toil, where the result of that lifetime of dissipation? I gave up everything, I denied nothing to the fire. What have I got now?—there came out this calf."

And does not a similar feeling come over us now sometimes when we have acquired at last that for which we have long laboured, and for which we have spent so much? It has been before us so long, we have reckoned so greatly on having perfect happiness when that is ours; let it be what it may, an innocent object or a sinful one, but one essentially earthly and transitory, when it is possessed, what, I ask, is the feeling that sweeps over the soul? Is it not, "I cast the gold into the fire, and there came out this calf?"

But oh! is not that a foretaste—faint indeed, but still one—of the sickening sensation at the last, when one truly sees what the gold is that has been cast away, and the calf has been broken to powder? Golden opportunities, golden time, golden talents, golden love, golden hopes,—all went into the fire, and there came out only this vile calf!

Point II. *Gold given to the Tabernacle.*

The converse of the above. Treasure laid up in heaven, sanctified by the Cloud of Glory, the Shekinah, resting upon it. Then when the LORD's House is revealed in its glory, then we shall see the gold we have stored up—our faculties, our time, our energies, our hearts' affections—all, all were given to that, to the Temple of GOD.

They too went into the fire, labour was borne, suffering was undergone, humiliations were submitted to—lost were they?

Listen! "Come, ye blessed of My FATHER, inherit the kingdom prepared for you from the foundation of the world." "Well done, good and faithful servants; ye have been faithful over few things, I will make you rulers over many things. Enter into the joy of your LORD."

XLII.

THE WORK OF CHRIST.

"*There was a little city, and few men within it; and there came a great king against it and besieged it, and built great bulwarks against it: now there was found in it a poor wise man, and he by his wisdom delivered the city; yet no man remembered that same poor man.*"—Eccles. ix. 14, 15.

Introduction. Nothing is known of the city or of the man; neither the time when the event occurred, nor the name of the city delivered, nor that of the man who delivered it, nor what were the means he used for his purpose. Why then is the story told? Here it is an illustration of the power of wisdom.

Subject. But it is a parable of the work of CHRIST.

Point I. The *little city* is this world; the *great king* is Satan, who assails it with all his power, and reduces it to great straits. The poor wise man is CHRIST: *poor*, having no place where to lay His head, ministered to by poor women of their substance; *wise*, oh! how wise! the Builder of the earth, the Eternal Wisdom itself incarnate.

By His wisdom *He delivered the city* from the enemy. By His death He overcame him that had the power of death; He delivered the world from the power of Satan, so that those therein were saved from falling into his slavery.

But no man remembered that same poor man. Is not that true?

Point II. But the parable has a further application.

Have we not been assailed by Satan, and has not CHRIST repeatedly delivered us? When our own power has been as nothing, and we have felt that he could reduce us at his will, has not the Poor Wise Man come to our aid and delivered us?

Did He not deliver us at our Baptism from the service of Satan? Has He not delivered us from the habits of sin when we have repented? When we were failing from want of nourishment, has He not opened the windows of heaven and rained bread upon us, that we might eat, and live, and be strong?

And have we remembered Him?

When temptation is passed, when trial and distress is over, have we not forgotten Him? When prosperity smiles and all is smooth, do we remember who stood in the boat and rebuked the winds and waves, and brought us to the shore? When we are full fed, have we not waxed fat and kicked?

Conclusion. There are two lessons, then, to be learnt from this parable:—

1. Not to despise the Wise Man or the means He uses, because He is poor, and they seem feeble. It is His Wisdom which has chosen them, and makes them mighty to work our deliverance.

2. When we are delivered, to remember Him and not fall into oblivion and ingratitude.

XLIII.

PENITENCE.

"*I rose up to open to my Beloved; and my hands dropped with myrrh, and my fingers with sweet smelling myrrh, upon the handles of the locks.*" —Song of Songs v. 5.

Introduction. The bride had been sitting in her room through the day. The sun had now set, the day was past, and a great void was in her heart. Presently she heard a step, and then a hand was put in through the hole of the door, and touched the handle. She rose up—it was the Bridegroom. But there was some hesitation. She had put off her dress—how should she put it on again? she had washed her feet—how should she defile them again by walking across the room?

She hesitated, I say; yet the Bridegroom called, "Open to Me, My sister, My love, My dove, My undefiled." She hesitated about her dress and her feet; and in the mean time the hand was withdrawn, and the steps went away.

Then she started up, forgetful of the dusty floor and her gay dress, and ran to the door, and put her hands on the lock which had been touched by the Beloved, and her hands dropped with myrrh, and her fingers with sweet-smelling myrrh, upon the handles of the locks.

Subject. *This is a picture of the soul aroused by Christ.*

I rose up, from indolence, from indifference, from a life of sin, from a half-hearted service, to strive, to seek, to follow, to find. Action comes first.

To open to my Beloved. The heart that had been closed He bids me open. He will not burst the door Himself; He puts in the pierced hand and calls, "Open to Me, My sister, My love, My dove, My undefiled!" He expects me to do something. I closed the door; I must unclose it.

Some darling sin keeps GOD out, as the small bolt holds the door shut; some small matter, may be, but it keeps the door shut, therefore it must be removed.

My hands dropped with myrrh .... upon the handles of the locks. This myrrh is contrition. Of myrrh there are two kinds—one is extracted by grinding, the other is the fluid myrrh, here rendered "sweet-smelling," and in the margin "passing," but which really means the exuding myrrh that flows from the plant itself.

Observe, we have in this passage, first the hands dropping with myrrh, that is, the ordinary, inferior, ground myrrh; then *my fingers with sweet-smelling myrrh*, or the fluid, superior myrrh which flows naturally. This succession expresses the growth of the soul in grace.

The myrrh is left by the Bridegroom, who puts His hand through the hole above the latch and touches the latch.

CHRIST gently puts His hand into the closed heart, through

some opening afforded by a calamity, a loss, a disappointment, a sorrow; and touches that which hinders Him from entering—touches the besetting sin, and leaves on it the myrrh of compunction.

Then the soul is stirred. It recognizes His voice, hastens to cast away the barrier, and first feels ordinary contrition, and then, as she becomes more in earnest, the naturally flowing bitterness of a true repentance. First she grieves from fear, then she is penitent through love.

Conclusion. Then the bride goes forth in pursuit of the Bridegroom. No more ease, indifference, closing of doors, and sleep; no more thought of the gay wedding robe, and of the dainty washed feet; in mean apparel, with bare feet bleeding on the stones, with anxious face, she pursues the Beloved, and follows where He leads. Is this not a picture? The penitent soul has now to take up its cross, and go and follow CHRIST through shame, and sorrow, and pain, if she would see Him, and clasp His feet, and possess Him for eternity.

XLIV.

WORSHIP.

"*O magnify the Lord our God, and worship Him upon His holy hill for the Lord our God is holy.*"—Ps. xcix. 9.

Introduction. People talk a great deal about "places of worship," "forms of worship," and so on; but do they understand what worship means? I think not, or they would use these expressions with greater care.

Ask So and so why she goes to church or chapel. She will say she likes the discourses, or the minister there. She goes to hear a sermon, and to "get good," to "feel good."

Now, worship does not mean hearing sermons, or getting good, or being made to feel good; it does not of necessity mean praying.

We hear a sermon or the Bible read to get instruction; we pray to get something. Now, worship does not mean *getting* anything at all—it means *giving* something. Worship no more means getting, than selling means buying.

Subject. *My subject then is Worship.* This will be our work for eternity, and the Bible tells us it is a work we must engage in, and learn to love on earth. What then does it mean?

I. *The offering of the mind.*

We offer the mind in meditation, when we withdraw our thoughts from this world, and from ourselves—we can be selfish even in prayer—when we gather in our attention, and concentrate it upon God, and God only.

The practice of meditation is not easy; for we are naturally prone to think of other things rather than God, but, just as God demands of us a portion of our time, and a portion of our means, so He requires of us an offering of our mind, by thinking at times of Him, and what His attributes are, or what He has done.

II. *The offering of the heart.*

We offer the heart in love; we exhibit our love in ardour of devotion, or in adorning the sanctuary, and making the service of the sanctuary beautiful. But love has a language of its own in which it speaks to God. Love must not be given wholly to things of this world. God must have an oblation of that also.

III. *The offering of the body.*

God made the mind, He therefore demands an offering of that; He made the heart, He requires that also; He made the body, He demands that the body shall join in worshipping Him. And this the body does by formal acts of bowing, kneeling, singing, and joining in the service of the Church, &c.

Remember God demands recognition as the Lord and Master and King of the whole man, body and soul, of man's mind, man's heart and man's body. Perfect worship is that in which all three unite; worship is imperfect when one or two exist, but the third factor drops out.

XLV.

PRAYER.

"*Open thy mouth wide and I will fill it.*"—Ps. lxxxi. 10.

Introduction. You see here a promise and a condition. It is so in all God's dealings with us. A promise of eternal life *if*——; a promise of protection *if*——; a promise of pardon for sin *if*——; a promise of grace *if*——. There is always something that we must do if we desire God to do anything for us.

Is it not so in the world? You are given abundant crops *if* you cultivate the soil; health, *if* you take care to avoid what is harmful; sufficiency, *if* you work for it; friendship, *if* you conciliate others.

Subject. *Well, the condition of receiving grace is prayer.*

Point I. God will not give to those who do not value His gifts. He requires you to need them, and needing them, to ask for them. He likens us to little birds who open their beaks, that their mother may feed them.

Dost thou need amendment of life? Open thy mouth wide, and I will fill it.

Dost thou need grace to break with a bad habit? Open thy mouth wide, and I will fill it.

Dost thou need strength to pass through a trial? Open thy mouth wide, and I will fill it.

Dost thou need special guidance in some difficulty? Open thy mouth wide, and I will fill it.

Dost thou want some special grace? Open thy mouth wide, and I will fill it.

Point II. If we had faith we should obtain more. We must ask, believing that we receive. This is much more difficult than we imagine. Generally we ask with a sort of hope that we shall get it, and if it does come, it is an agreeable surprise; we take all the if's into consideration, and count chances, when we pray; sometimes even we think the thing will happen whether we pray or not, so we will just ask, it can do no harm.

Now there is no faith in that. "Ask, nothing doubting," ask, with the full certainty that you will get it. This sort of faith grows, and nothing is more wonderful in the lives of the saints than their confidence in prayer, and the way in which they always got what they wanted, because they asked, never doubting for an instant that they would have it.

Conclusion. A traveller in the Alps offered some money to a peasant who had shown him his way. The man shook his head. The traveller, thinking the sum was considered insufficient, doubled it. Again the man shook his head. "I cannot take it," said he, "*I have got no pocket.*"

How often must not this be said of you! You have no

means of keeping the precious gifts of GOD. "Come !" says He, "I offer the waters of life freely." You cannot receive them—you have no pocket. "Come that I may give thee pardon for thine offences !" No pardon can you accept—you have no pocket. "Come, My Body is broken, My Blood is outpoured, eat and drink and live for ever." You cannot draw near, you shrink from the invitation, because you know you have no pocket. In vain He offers His abundant grace, pardon to the sinner, strength to the feeble, rest to the weary, meat to the hungry ; in vain His priceless treasures are spread before thankless hearts—they cannot, will not receive them—they have no pocket.

XLVI.

THANKSGIVING.

"*Hezekiah rendered not again according to the benefit done unto him : for his heart was lifted up ; and therefore there was wrath upon him.*"—2 Chron. xxxii. 25.

Introduction. What was it that had lifted up the heart of Hezekiah ? We read, verses 27—30 : "He prospered in all his works." Why ? "GOD gave him substance very much."

Subject. *Thanksgiving is a necessity*, to keep alive our consciousness of dependence upon GOD.

Point I. GOD visits in mercy. People forget this. When a man falls dead ; when a rich man is ruined ; when a nation is humbled, people talk of it as GOD's visitation.

If corn crops go on right, if trade prospers, we attribute it to the soil and weather, or to our skilful speculation. But if there comes a hail-storm, or a fire consuming our stock, at once—it is GOD's visitation.

Do you think GOD only visits the earth to curse it? David thought differently, "Thou visitest the earth and blessest it; Thou makest it very plenteous." Every blade of corn grows by the visitation of GOD. People talk of GOD as if they saw only His majesty as a retributive justice; but He waters the hills from above. (Read Ps. 104.)

Point II. Gratitude therefore is due to Him for all His mercy that He exerts day by day. Hezekiah had received, he rendered not in return the thanks that were due to GOD. The Jews received abundant blessings, they rendered not a return, and were cast off.

Indeed it is a law of nature that return must be made.

The seas receive the rivers and return the clouds; the earth receives the grain, and dressing, and returns the harvest; the flower is given water, and it returns its fragrant scent.

It is true that we can, of ourselves, make no adequate return, but a means has been provided us for making one, which is an equivalent to all blessings accorded us. This means is in the Eucharist.

℣. Lift up your hearts.

℟. We lift them up unto the LORD.

℣. Let us give thanks unto our LORD GOD.

℟. It is meet and right so to do.

It is very meet, right, and our bounden duty that we should at all times and in all places give thanks unto Thee, O FATHER, almighty, everlasting GOD. Therefore with angels and archangels, and with all the company of heaven, we laud and magnify Thy glorious Name, evermore praising Thee, and saying, Holy, holy, holy, LORD GOD of Hosts, heaven and earth are full of Thy glory: Glory be to Thee, O LORD most high.

XLVII.

ADVANCE.

"*Friend, go up higher.*"—S. Luke xiv. 10.

Introduction. Paraphrase of the Parable.

Subject. Its lesson is double. (1) Humility, and (2) Obedience to GOD's call. Now there are two very great dangers, against which this parable cautions us, and it is of these I shall now speak. (1) Setting our religious profession above our life, and (2) Setting our religious profession below our life.

Point I. *Setting our religious profession above our life.* That is, taking the upper place when properly we should occupy a lower one. As communicating too frequently, when we are not careful in self-examination and self-discipline; being too demonstrative in Church, when our lives are somewhat careless and ease-loving; making too loud a talk of religion, when we never deny ourselves in meat or drink, or by crossing our wills.

There is, of course, a worse form of this, which is hypocrisy.

A countryman once gave an usurer a piece of gold to change. The usurer took some silver and began, "In the name of GOD, blessed Mary, and all the Saints, four, five, six." The countryman noticed that by this means he received the amount in silver minus three pieces. Therefore he said, "I will trouble you to leave GOD, the blessed Mary, and the Saints out this time in your counting; begin again."

I think a great many, if not guilty of downright conscious

hypocrisy, put in GOD, and blessed Mary, and the Saints when they much better had not, and make the names cover a sad deficiency in their own lives. If they would only talk less of religious matters, and practise the first principles of honour, truth, and straight-forwardness, it would be much better.

Point II. *Setting our religious profession below our life.*

This is quite as common an error as the other. When GOD has distinctly called us, and we refuse to go higher—refuse, that is, to take a higher and closer walk with GOD, when we know He expects it. Living a steady, moral life, but not being a communicant. Having a consciousness of sin and yet not seeking relief from it in confession.

All our life is one of growth—our faith, our hope, our love.

Catholic doctrine is full of mysteries, and faith rises to new and newer horizons. Those who see less than others should seek to rise, not disparage those truths beheld by those more gifted, they should seek to make faith go up higher, behold more, and believe more. And so with love; our love is capable of growth if exercised. We should try to go up higher in our charity, to love GOD better, and have a less selfish love of men.

Conclusion. Never let us be contented to profess less than we are capable of holding; and whenever we feel a call to move up, let us obey at once, and soar to a higher and truer faith, a clearer hope, a more abounding charity, and these we shall find in a closer walk with GOD. Take a low room, but do not remain in it; the call sounds through life, Advance, Excelsior! Friend, go up higher!

XLVIII.

DELAY.

"*A time to get and a time to lose.*"—Eccles. iii. 6.

Introduction. Does not Solomon in these words sum up what man's life is? It is a time to get grace, and get heaven; it is also a time to lose grace, to throw away chances and to lose heaven.

It is a time to get more knowledge, more experience, more prudence, more reality, more reverence, more love of truth; it is a time to lose the faculties given us by nature, by wasting opportunities, not educating our powers, and dissipating our talents.

Man's life is made up of opportunities. Opportunities arise—some come as it were by chance, others man may make for himself. Shall he catch and utilize them, or shall he let them slip, and lose them for ever?

Subject. *I am going to speak of delay in taking hold of opportunities, and thus allowing them to elude our grasp.*

Point I. There was once a countryman who set out to visit a town in which he hoped to find work. He had lived on a heath where there was no river. He reached the banks of one on his way, and was astonished. He sought not to ford it, or go round by a bridge, or call a boat, but he sat down to wait till the water ran away.

Now too many act like that clown on their way to the eternal city: across their path lie difficulties—they sit down and wait till the difficulties pass.

One man waits for youth and the heat of passion to pass,

another till he is comfortably settled, another till some trouble is over, another till some affair in which he is interested is terminated, before they advance on their heavenward way.

They wait for every obstacle to their salvation to be removed, yet obstacles are continually succeeding one another as the waves of the river, and form an everlasting stream, whose source is never dried up.

Point II. Opportunities of good, moreover, are allowed to slip away. For instance, the opportunity of training up a child in the way he should go, till it be too late, the opportunity neglected through overmuch love and carelessness—it was so with Eli and his sons.

Or an opportunity of repentance and amendment presents itself. The heart is softened by a sermon, or by some bereavement, or by some humiliation, and it feels its need of repentance; but this is delayed, and the desire passes away—it was so with Felix.

Or an opportunity of doing some right and good act presents itself suddenly, and through timidity and fear of man it is allowed to escape past recall—it was so with Pilate when trying CHRIST.

Conclusion. Remember the promptitude of Peter; when he had sinned, and was conscious of his sin, *at once* he rose up and went forth and wept bitterly.

Remember Abimelech; when he was nearly falling unconsciously into sin, he rose up *at once* in the night, and did justice and put the temptation from him.

XLIX.

EARTHLY IDOLS.

"*Ye have taken away my gods which I made, and ye are gone away: and what have I more?*"—Judges xviii. 24.

Introduction. The story of Micah losing his idol, and then having nothing. The story of a martyr despoiled by men of everything, but they cannot rob him of his GOD, and that is to him all in all.

Subject. *I am going to speak of earthly idols.*

Point I. What are those things on which we have set our hearts? They are our idols—gods that we have often ourselves made. To them we have sacrificed everything, on them we have pinned our happiness. We lose them suddenly, and then—"what have I more?"

Say that worldly goods have been the idol; on money the whole heart is set. Suddenly it takes to itself wings, I have lost it, "and what have I more?" Or it is some dear wife, or darling child, engrossing all my thoughts. Death comes and sweeps it away, "and what have I more?" Or it is reputation—I have toiled to acquire that; suddenly it is lost, I am heartbroken, I cared so wholly for that, "and what have I more?"

Point II. But take from a Christian all, and you only attach him nearer to his GOD. You cannot rob him of his GOD.

Take from me my house, my subsistence, my health, my family, and do you ask me, "What have I more?"

What have I more!—I have my GOD, who is my treasure,

who is my food and sustenance, who is the strength of my health, who is father, mother, and brother to me.

What have I more!—I have the Blood of JESUS to cleanse me, the Body of JESUS to satisfy me.

What have I more!—I have eternal life as my prize, the Holy City as my home eternal in the heavens, and the certainty of waking up after CHRIST'S likeness, and of being satisfied therewith.

L.

ADVENT.—THE WATCHER ON THE WALLS.

"*Watchman, what of the night? Watchman, what of the night? The watchman said, The morning cometh.*"—Isa. xxi. 11, 12.

Introduction. Of old GOD called His prophets to be watchmen to His people. Isaiah says that GOD declared, "I have set watchmen on thy walls, O Jerusalem;" and Jeremiah, "I set watchmen over you, saying, Hearken to the sound of the trumpet;" and Ezekiel, "Son of man, I have made thee a watchman unto the house of Israel; therefore hear the word at My mouth, and give them warning from Me." And now, under the new dispensation, the preachers of GOD'S Word take the place of the prophets, relieving them on their guard. The older prophets looked for the dawn of CHRIST'S first coming, we for the daybreak of His Second Advent. They watched through the night of the old covenant broken by Israel, we through that of the new dispensation, rejected by the world.

Subject. It is a striking picture this of watchmen. It represents a city crowning the hills, girded with walls and towers. And all lights are out as the night approaches its close. For the first few hours the lights in the houses are many, and the streets are thronged; as night crept on, all grew more hushed, and the lights were fewer, and the darkness deeper. The watchers standing at the parapets, or pacing up and down, count the wheeling stars, and see that the city is buried in sleep.

See! high up in yonder attic, a feeble glimmer from the candle where is a sick person awake in pain. There a faint glow through the church window, where the perpetual lamp burns before the Blessed Sacrament. Now the windows of the convent flash alight, as the religious come to Prime and Lauds.

So hour by hour steals by, and the watchers are weary, and lean over the battlements with wistful gaze directed eastward, expecting the dawn. Presently there is a greyness over the eastern hills, and the horizon looks blacker than heretofore. Then a thread of light runs along the ragged fringe of mountain. The watchman nearest east lifts his horn, and blows a blast which echoes through the sleeping city. Hark! it is answered by one after another. And now there is a stir in the city. Some wake, but others sleep. Some lights are kindled, others are still dark. There is a movement in the street, the light grows, and the church bells chime for morning prayer.

Application. This is the picture. Surely it is a type, and that a very significant one. That long night of darkness, of Christ's withdrawal of His visible Presence, is it not a time for spiritual sleep? At first many lights burn, but the number of watchers, the number of those whose light shines forth before men decreases, till only a few are found, few and far between, who "prevent the daybreak." From out the watch-towers of the Church the trumpet peals, calling to the sleeper to awake and arise from the dead, that CHRIST may give him light. And the consciousness of the Coming is present amongst many, and they awake, and trim their lamps and prepare.

O my brethren! you who pass your time in ease, you who dream away your hours in pleasure, awake! the dawn is at hand. You who make no effort to secure your salvation, who let the years pass without formal and complete reconciliation with your GOD, awake! the dawn is at hand. You who listen drowsily to the watchers' Advent call, and turn again on your couch, awake! the dawn is at hand!

LI.

ADVENT—THE PERPETUITY OF THE CHURCH.

"*Verily I say unto you, This generation shall not pass away till all be fulfilled. Heaven and earth shall pass away: but My words shall not pass away.*"—S. Luke xxi. 32, 33 (Gospel for the Second Sunday in Advent.)

Introduction. Our LORD has been describing the Judgment, and the signs preceding it, in sun and moon and stars. He has spoken of the distress of nations, the sea and waves roaring, men's hearts failing them for fear, of the shaking of the powers of heaven. Everything seems disturbed, dislocated, in movement. Then He adds a word of consolation. Notwithstanding this general convulsion and disorder, one thing will remain firm and unaltered, one thing will not be shaken and thrown down. "This generation shall not pass away." And to give greater confidence, He adds the solemn promise, "Heaven and earth shall pass away: but My words shall not pass away." And you will observe, to show the gravity and importance of this promise, He prefixes to it the "verily" which always goes before the unfolding of a great and mysterious truth.

Point I. *What this promise does not signify.*

It is evident from the context that this promise is given as something which is to sustain and cheer His faithful, it is something to assure them in the midst of all the signs and wonders.

Literally, that generation did pass away, and the end was not, if we take generation as the race of men then living. It has been supposed by some that CHRIST was speaking only of the destruction of Jerusalem, which took place in the year 70, some fifty years later; but that would hardly be a fulfilment of the promise, nor did that event prove a redemption to the Christians, which should make them lift up their heads with joy; nor indeed can our LORD's words be made to apply to this alone, without great contraction and allowance for poetical language. Undoubtedly, giving them their obvious meaning, they refer to the Judgment, and the promise "This generation shall not pass away," was intended as an assurance which should give great confidence to His elect, looking for the coming of that Great Day.

Point II. *What the promise does signify.*

A father begets a son in his own image, and the son inherits the life, and faculties, and energy of the father; the life is committed from father to son, from generation to generation, entire and unimpaired. This is natural generation.

So is there a spiritual generation. CHRIST ordained one in His Church, a generation of the faithful. Its powers, graces, its divine life, never die out; it has lived through ages of persecution, and it lives still, and will live till all is fulfilled.

CHRIST imparted to His infant Church certain gifts. He gave it the Spirit to vivify it, Sacraments to sustain the union between Himself and the members, and officers to rule His kingdom and dispense His sacraments.

Did this generation pass away with the first Apostles? No. Fresh members were baptized into it, fresh priests were ordained to supply the members with the Living Bread, fresh bishops were consecrated, to commission the priests in their several posts.

Point III. *This generation is indestructible.*

In natural generation a family may die out. But not so in the spiritual generation. The life of the Catholic Church is divine, and what is divine is eternal. Other bodies of Christians may and must fail—witness the old sects and newer dissenting bodies changing and disappearing. But—and remember, this is our great hope and rock of confidence—the Church, the spiritual generation, cannot fail. Baptism will still regenerate, Absolution will still cleanse, Confirmation will still strengthen, the Eucharist will still feed, ministerial grace will still be given in Orders, as at the beginning, unaltered, undiminished, till CHRIST comes in glory.

Conclusion. This then is the hope and encouragement held out in the text. Our LORD says, The end is coming. Kingdoms shall fall into ruin, society shall break up, disorder will invade all relations of man with man. There will be an upheaval of the foundations of civilized life, but —My Church and My Sacraments will remain unaltered, My Kingdom constituted as of old, My Sacraments ever grace-giving.

LII.

ADVENT.—THE OPENING OF THE EYES AT DEATH.

"*In that day shall the deaf hear the words of the book, and the eyes of the blind shall see out of obscurity and out of darkness.*"—Isa. xxix. 18.

Introduction. What can be a blind man's idea of things he has never seen, a deaf man's of things he has never heard? The story is told of a youth who had never seen, but an operation was performed, and a glimpse of light entered his eyes, before the bandages were put on, to be continued for several days. He was found after this constantly sobbing, and when at last asked the reason, he said, "I saw for a moment what light was, and now I fear lest it should be denied me to see it always."

Subject. Now there is a moment when every eye will be opened, and every ear will be unstopped; when the veil is withdrawn from the eye and it sees all clearly, and the ear hears all distinctly.

I. A man is returning from a public house at night. He has to cross a lock. The fumes of liquor are in his head. He trolls snatches of comic songs and repeats low jests. His feet are on the lock. A totter, a fall, a splash heard by none, one sharp cry in the night, a battle with the black water, a roar in his ears, a fire in his brain, a gasping for breath, a loss of consciousness—the point of the joke is gone, the chorus of the song is forgotten, the red faces round the tavern fire no more remembered, all begins to fade and grow fainter, colours to disappear in grey, forms to lose themselves in mist—then, suddenly, a flash of light, and all is clear. The soul has broken loose from the body; it quivers a moment above that white face looking up into the black sky, and now "the eyes of the blind see out of obscurity," and the ears hear—what do they see, what do they hear?

II. *The eyes see the past life unrolled.* They behold the first little forgotten sins, the boyish acts of wilfulness unrebuked, which happened so long ago; those first threads of the black pattern which has coloured and penetrated the texture of his life. They see each act of intemperance, every deed of violence, every yielding to lust, every fraudulent action, every brutal blow to wife and child. The ears are opened, and they hear every word that has been spoken, the gossiping speech, the slander, the lie, the foul expression, the curse, the oath, the blasphemy.

They see God upon His throne, seated amidst the glories of heaven, angels gathered around Him, saints bowed in adoration, elders casting their crowns at His feet. Paradise spread before, its grassy flats traversed by happy throngs of ransomed ones. They see Satan triumphant, standing up to record before God the evil deeds of that unhappy soul. They see the guardian angel weeping, with drooping wings, and the scroll of that soul's good deeds a blank from end to end. What is there to plead against the accusing angel? One struggle for amendment to cast into the scale?—There is none. One prayer for grace to overcome?—There is none. One desire for something better?—There is none. One tear of contrition at that supreme moment when the waters closed?—Not one. Then the ears that would be deaf hear the words of the Book, the words of condemnation.

Conclusion. Oh my brethren, let this thought be impressed upon us:—Our eyes will be opened one day to see our lives in all their reality, without the excuses and glosses we cast over our actions, our ears will hear the words of the Book from which judgment will be given, which judgment will be very righteous, very just.

LIII.

ADVENT.

"*Comfort ye, comfort ye My people, saith your God. Speak ye comfortably to Jerusalem.*"—Isa. xl. 1, 2.

Introduction. These words were addressed in prophecy to S. John the Baptist, previous to CHRIST'S manifestation of Himself. He was to go to desolate, weeping Israel, and to cry to her, that her warfare was accomplished, that her iniquity was pardoned, that the glory of the LORD was about to be revealed, that the LORD would come with a strong hand, His reward with Him, to feed His flock like a shepherd, and to gather the lambs with His arm.

Subject. But it applies principally to the second coming of CHRIST; a coming to those who are not Israel after the flesh, to those who are indeed His people, to the true Jerusalem, His Church.

Point I. Throughout the Christian world at present unquestionably there is—deep down in the hearts of those living nearest to GOD, in many a convent and monastery, where no sound is heard save prayer and praise, in the stillness of some hearts which have never known aught of life save that which is hid in CHRIST with GOD—there is, I say, a yearning after CHRIST'S second coming, a strange presentiment that not very long time will pass, ere the wheels of His chariot will be heard, that ere long He will heal the breaches of Zion, and speak comfortably to poor Jerusalem, "when Ephraim shall not envy Judah, and Judah shall not vex Ephraim."

Point II. And surely now the Church needs comfort, for the Christian world is getting further from CHRIST. Infidelity is general everywhere. Those who hold portions of the truth revile and separate themselves from those who hold it in its entirety. There is a general envy and jealousy of GOD, a grudging Him the honour due to His name. The graces of the Church are fading, her beauties are withering, her tears are on her cheek, she sits as a widow and weeps, her children are estranged from her, and there is coldness among those who remain with her. Why does He tarry who bears the balm of Gilead?

Point III. It is not to all that the words "Comfort ye, comfort ye My people," are spoken. Not even to all the baptized, though all these are, in one sense, the people of GOD. But there is a great division among the baptized. There are the faithful and the unfaithful, those who try to keep the covenant, and those who do not.

The words are addressed to those who are truly "My people," to those who have either never left the covenant, or who have returned to it. How can I speak comfortably to those who are out of covenant? Shall I speak comfortably to formal Christians, to those who cloke a worldly heart with a profession of religion, to those who thrust themselves into the holiest places, but are all the while sensual? No, I speak comfortably to the real Christian, to him who believes and trusts, to him who laments and bewails his sins, to him who sorrows at his own imperfection, to him whose daily life is a warfare, to him who grieves for the distracted state of the Church, who mourns over its worldliness, over the heresy that has invaded our branch of it, its bondage, the insults offered it, the little head religion makes against the powers of darkness. To all such as weep and suffer for the cause of CHRIST, the words come, "Comfort ye, comfort ye My people, saith your GOD."

LIV.

CHRISTMAS.

"*The Word was made Flesh.*"—S. John i. 14.

Introduction. I wonder whether you have ever tried to realise what is the real significance of Christmas teaching?

Anciently it was said that contradictories mutually excluded one another. Christmas Day is the negation of that axiom, it teaches us the conciliation of contradictory propositions. For CHRIST in One person unites and reconciles the finite and the infinite, mortality and immortality, the limited and the unlimited. He is it once omnipresent and in the crib of Bethlehem, almighty and a feeble infant, eternal and brief-lived,—in a word, He is GOD and Man.

Point I. *Why was Christ incarnate?*

The angels answer, "Glory to GOD in the highest." Yes, for the glory of GOD, GOD took flesh; for the glory of GOD is the happiness of His creatures.

What is it that Angels seek? The glory of GOD.

For what was man made? For the glory of GOD.

What was the Fall? Man seeking himself instead of GOD—seeking himself in ignorance, not knowing that man's happiness is alone to be found in glorifying GOD.

Why was GOD incarnate? To lead man back to GOD, to bring him out of self-seeking into self-devotion to GOD, and in such self-devotion to the glory of GOD to find his happiness once more.

Festivals lose half their joyousness and half their significance when we regard them merely from a selfish point of view, as:—what benefit we can derive from them, what moral lessons do they convey to us? They were chiefly instituted to glorify GOD, to make us forget ourselves, in seeking the honour of our All in All.

Do you think angels in heaven praise GOD because they get something by it? that the elders offer their odours calculating what profit will accrue to them? that the saints strike their harps hoping to be paid by the hour? No, no, the motive of action in heaven is the glory of GOD, and such should be our motive on earth for keeping festival.

Point II. *How can we seek God's glory?*

By self-forgetfulness. The god and tyrant of this world is not Satan. He has retired of late into the background, and left the field open for one who does his work a great deal more thoroughly, and not half so clumsily—the great god SELF. Self dethrones GOD, self makes us covet everything, and grudge GOD all. What is the Protestant prejudice against Catholic worship, but Self impatient of honour and glory and splendour being offered to GOD, grudging them because it craves them all for its own glorification.

GOD's glory is to be sought in the utter destruction of the self, by giving up self for GOD, by dethroning self from its niche on the altar, for, believe me, religion, with too many, is only sanctified selfishness.

CHRIST sought our happiness, let us seek His glory,—and in seeking His glory we shall find perfect happiness.

Conclusion. How bounteous is CHRIST, how niggard are we! He gives us all, we are reluctant to surrender to Him anything; He is full of love, we are cold; He humble, we proud.

Let us seek the glory of GOD, and we shall find peace on earth and goodwill extended to us.

LV.

NEW YEAR.

"*I will go out, as at other times before, and shake myself. And he wist not that the Lord was departed from him.*"—Judges xvii. 20.

Introduction. We have done with the old year. Its bright sunshine, its happiness, its green fields and flowers, its sorrows, its falls, its trials,—all are over. And the sky has flung a pall of white over the earth to bury the past. Now a new year begins. Three hundred and sixty-five days of sun, twelve months, and four seasons, as of old—the same thing over again—but how will they be spent?

Subject. Let me urge you to make a struggle to break from bad habits for once and for all.

Point I. *Case of Samson.*

Samson loved the treacherous Delilah, who was in league with his enemies, seeking his destruction. Samson knew this, or might have known it, had he not been blinded by passion or self-confidence. He lay with his head on her lap, and she bound him with seven green withs, because he said that if so bound his strength would depart from him. Then she called his foes, but he shook himself and broke the withs. She tried the same treachery with seven new ropes. Then again with weaving the seven locks of his head, and fastening them to a beam.

If ever a man was given evidence of the treachery of one in whom he placed confidence, Samson was that man. Yet he actually trusted her a fourth time, and this time with the true secret of his strength. She shaved his head as he slept, and then called the Philistines upon him.

He woke and said, "I will go out, as at other times before, and shake myself." But he was too late, he had gone too far, trusted Delilah once too often, and now "the Lord was departed from him."

Now, my brethren, is not this like too many of you? You go on falling under temptation again and again, voluntarily surrendering yourself without a struggle, and when sin has been committed, "I will go out, as at other times before, and shake myself." There is no compunction, no resolution of amendment, no determination to break with the besetting sin, to withdraw from the evil surroundings, "I will go out, as at other times before, and shake myself," and then return to the lap of Delilah, and yield without difficulty or fear to her treachery.

Point II. *This may take place once too often.*

Remember, after Samson had been warned three times, God strove with him no more; he rose from his sin, thinking he would shake himself, "but he wist not that the Lord was departed from him."

And do not we too often regard our sins lightly, and just shake ourselves, with a light contrition, and half-hearted confession—with no firm set determination to amend? Then I tell you, there must be an end of this easygoing repentance. GOD will not endure this shaking of yourself, and returning as dogs to your vomit. Beware, as you value your souls, how you trifle with sin, how you regard temptation lightly. Once more, and the patience of the Almighty may be at an end, and you may purpose to go out as at other times before and shake yourself, but alas! the LORD will have departed from you for ever.

LVI.

THE EPIPHANY.

"*We have seen His star, and are come to worship Him.*"—S. Matth. ii. 2.

Introduction. Perhaps no incident in the Gospel is so strange, so singular in its picturesqueness, so wondrously beautiful as this of the coming of the three kings, guided by a star, to the place where Mary sits with her Divine Child on her lap.

The three kings are emblematical of the great races of mankind, descended from Shem, Ham, and Japheth, drawing near to bend before the Incarnate GOD, and offer Him their treasures.

Point I. *They followed the guiding star, which led them to Jesus.*

We too have JESUS as the object of our journey. Through the long course of life, we have one hope, to see GOD face to face, and to live in the light of His countenance; not content with seeing Him, by faith, through the veil of Sacraments, we look forward with desire to behold Him as He is, to know even as we are known.

Why is it that we are content to suffer here, that we are satisfied to endure loss here? Because we hope to see CHRIST and be repaid by Him when life's journey is over.

Point II. *We also have a guiding star.*

First, we have natural reason—that which guided the good and wise of the old heathen world, and which directs the heathen, the unbeliever, and the heretic at present. It is not a perfect light, it is uncertain and not steady, but it is all that some have to trust to, and it is infinitely better than none at all.

Secondly, revealed religious truth. Before CHRIST came, men were in ignorance as to what GOD was, what He desired of men, what was His nature, and what was man's hope beyond the grave. Natural reason felt after these things, but failed to discover them; then CHRIST came and revealed what men desired to know. He showed them what was the nature of GOD, what are His laws, and what will be man's lot, if he keeps or breaks these laws.

This is the true star that guides Christians—a star far more clear, and far more constant, than natural reason.

Conclusion. And now, what made the kings follow the star? Earnest desire of attaining the Truth.

I speak with sorrow. How few are to be seen making the smallest effort to follow the guiding star. It points the way, but only one here, and another there, shakes off his torpor to arise and follow. What advance is there to note? What increase of holiness, love of GOD, and zeal is there to be found?

The light shines, every day clearer, but none follow—

why? Because the god of this world hath blinded their eyes. There is no reality in people now-a-days, our civilization is a varnish, and we grow to believe in glosses and makeshifts, and show and pretence—reality is love of Truth, unreality is indifference to Truth.

As long as men love not truth for truth's sake, the light may shine, the star may point, but none will follow.

LVII.

FIRST SUNDAY AFTER THE EPIPHANY.

"*His mother kept all these sayings in her heart.*"—S. Luke ii. 51.

Introduction. In God's Word we find rules of life for all conditions of men, for all stages of life, for all positions in society. The Word of God is a mirror, into which man may look to see how he should live and act. The Gospel for this day gives instruction to several grades of men.

I. *Parents are taught*—

1. To train up their children in the fear and admonition of the Lord; to bring them at an early hour to the temple; to train them to love its courts, to delight in its services.

2. To seek the wandering, and bring them back; to seek them anxiously and sorrowing, should they have strayed into heresy or sin.

II. *Children are taught*—

1. To seek the paths of righteousness and the way of God, even though against their parents' wishes. "He that loveth father or mother more than Me, is not worthy of Me."

2. In all else, to be subject to parents. GOD humbled Himself to obey Mary and Joseph, and children must take from Him a pattern of obedience.

III. *Married persons are taught—*

1. To feel for each other, and sympathize with each other. JESUS was not the son of Joseph, yet Joseph accompanied Mary in her search.

2. To show deference to one another. Mary said, "Thy father and I have sought Thee sorrowing," placing Joseph in honour before herself.

IV. *Priests are taught—*

To abide continually in the temple hearing the doubts and difficulties of others, and answering them as GOD gives them understanding.

V. *Finally, All are taught—*

1. Not to let vain excuses hinder them from coming to Church. For Mary and Joseph came notwithstanding Archelaus, and left their home trusting GOD's promise that no ill should befall it. (Exod. xxxiv.)

2. CHRIST listened humbly to the doctors, although He knew all things. So let men listen to the preacher, and not puff themselves up in their superior knowledge. They can take the text and practise patience.

3. Mary, Joseph, and JESUS accomplished the days—a lesson to people not to be too eager to get out of Church before service is over, in the midst of the Celebration of the Blessed Sacrament, or to be too eager for the close of Lent, or any other season of fasting and self-denial.

4. To deal liberally and cheerfully with GOD. It is the mark of a servile mind to grudge doing more than is laid down by the law. The law did not require women and children to go up to Jerusalem.

5. CHRIST is said to have increased in favour with GOD and man. So let us seek first the favour of GOD, and the favour of man will be added to us. But if we seek the favour of man first, we shall lose the favour of GOD.

LVIII.

SECOND SUNDAY AFTER THE EPIPHANY.

"*There were set there six waterpots of stone.*"—S. John ii. 6.

Introduction. There were six waterpots from which, this day, good wine was poured out. And there are as many persons, or groups of persons, from which we may take pattern.

For us did Isaiah prophesy, "With joy shall ye draw water out of the wells of salvation." (Isa. xii. 3.) These wells are the doctrine, the example, the miracles, the parables of CHRIST. Do ye drink with joy, for though we, the ministers of the Bridegroom, may seem to pour forth to you only water, yet if you receive it in CHRIST'S name, it will be converted into the wine of precious doctrine, refreshing and strengthening your souls.

I. *Christ.* From His example we learn—

1. That He is our helper in time of need. He suffers us to fall into necessity and perplexity, that we may learn to rely, not on earth, but on heaven. Therefore He postponed performing this miracle till all seemed lost. He woke not to deliver His disciples till the ship began to sink. He healed not the woman with the issue of blood, till she had

spent all her substance on doctors; He rescued not the Three Children, till they were in the fire; nor Susanna, till she was led to death.

2. Notice how liberally CHRIST succours, not giving a small amount, but six waterpots containing two or three firkins apiece. So He gives ever abundantly, more than He is asked for. When He fed the people in the wilderness, there were twelve basketfuls of fragments left.

II. *Mary.* From her we learn—

1. To have constant hope. Our LORD spake roughly to her, yet she persisted, bidding the servants obey. So must we not weary in prayer. GOD delays answering, to make us persevere.

2. That GOD needs not enticing words of man's wisdom in prayer, but the plain outspoken utterance of a need. "They have no wine."

3. That we should feel solicitude for others. Mary asked, out of a kindly sympathy with the perplexity of the host.

III. *Disciples.* From them we learn—

Faith. "His disciples," we are told, "believed on Him." And yet this was the first miracle He had performed.

IV. *Bride and Bridegroom* set an example of Moderation.

They provided scarce enough wine. Let Christian feasting be temperate, with no excess in eating and drinking, then will not CHRIST be absent from the board, but will with His Presence consecrate the happy banquet.

V. *The Ruler of the Feast.*

From his words we learn that it is the way of the world to give what is good first, but "when men have well drunk" that which is inferior. The world gives pleasures which end in bitterness; prosperity, but afterwards pain and death.

But on the other hand, God gives what is inferior first, and keeps the best to the last. Now He gives us trial, but hereafter reward. "Remember that thou in thy lifetime receivedst thy good things, and likewise Lazarus evil things, but now he is comforted, and thou art tormented."

VI. Lastly, *the Servants* teach us the nature of true obedience.

1. It is *unquestioning*. They did not stop to argue the uselessness of filling the pitchers, but obeyed without dispute.

2. It was *prompt*. "Fill the waterpots," and they did so at once. "Draw out and bear to the ruler," and they did so.

3. It was *exact*. "Fill the waterpots," and they filled them to the brim.

4. It was *voluntary*, for Christ and His Mother had no authority over them. They were not their masters, yet they cheerfully obeyed.

LIX.

SEPTUAGESIMA.

"*The kingdom of heaven is like unto a man that is an householder, which went out early in the morning to hire labourers into his vineyard. And when he had agreed with the labourers for a penny a day, he sent them into his vineyard.*"—S. Matth. xx. 1, 2.

Introduction. The time of festivity is over. Christmas and Epiphany carols are put aside, Alleluia is banished from our Churches. The festive evergreens are removed; for to-day the Church strikes another note than that of joy.

with the assistance of the Holy Ghost. Do we love the things that are good, and holy, and pure? Do we seek first the kingdom of God and His righteousness? Do we delight in the law of God after the inward man? Do we find His yoke easy, and His burden light? Or does the spirit revolt, do flesh and blood struggle and oppose themselves, and the will fight against the pure and perfect will of God?

This, my brethren, must be learned by self-examination.

Point III. *The Consequence.*

If our heart be right with Christ's Heart we will give Him our hand and be admitted into His chariot. He will join Himself to us, and make us sharers in His triumph. "Give Me thy hand," He says, "give it Me in confidence. Of thyself I know that thou canst do nothing, that thou art weak, therefore have I thrust out My hand in sacraments to hold thee up and to lift thee into My chariot. Fear Me not, give Me thy hand, My grace is sufficient for thee."

Conclusion. Let the sacred Heart of the ascended Jesus be our study, that we may conform our heart to it.

Consider its charity, its purity, its self-devotion. O Lord, make, I pray Thee, my heart right with Thine Heart, that I may go forth to meet Thee, and accept Thy Hand, and, feeling Thy strength, may be stayed up and enter into Thy chariot, and so go on with Thee to Thy city of Jerusalem, to Thy triumph and Thy glory.

LXXVI.

WHITSUN-DAY.

"*Let Thy loving Spirit lead me forth into the land of righteousness.*"—Ps. cxliii. 10.

Introduction. When Elijah ascended into Heaven, he left behind him with Elisha a double measure of his spirit.

Our Master has gone up on high. He has entered into the Heaven of heavens; yet, ere He left, He communicated His authority to His apostles, His mantle fell on them, and this day He gives them, in abundant measure, His Spirit.

Now will His "loving Spirit lead them forth into the land of righteousness," and not lead them only, but us also, for the Spirit given on the first Whitsun-Day dwells still in the Church, the sap of every plant that God hath planted, the life-breath of every soul into which God hath breathed.

Let Thy loving Spirit. This is addressed to God the Father, from Whom the Spirit proceeds, or to God the Son, Who sends the Comforter. Truly may that Spirit be designated "loving," for He is the Fount of Love, the Well-spring of Charity, the Author of Good. Loving us, in that through Him, Mary became the Mother of Jesus, our Incarnate God, loving us, in that He has come down to rest on the Church, loving us, in that He descends on every Christian new-born in the regenerating stream.

Lead me forth; forth, that is, out of sin, out of old bad habits, forth from my miserable self, from my weakness, coldness, faithlessness; forth from the old Adam, that I may put on the new man. "The Spirit helpeth our infirmities," driving away ignorance, strengthening the will to follow the good, steeling the heart against the evil, helping the memory to recall GOD's mercies.

Without this leading we must fail. The apostles were ignorant fishermen, and now the Spirit of Wisdom has descended on them, they by their eloquence convert thousands. They were timid, forsaking their LORD, and denying Him; and now, endowed with the Spirit of Fortitude, they are ready to endure bonds, and imprisonment, and death also for His Name's sake.

Into the land of righteousness. The land flowing with milk and honey, the land where all is safe, hope is fulfilled, faith beholds all plain, and love is ever burning. A land of righteousness, for CHRIST, the King of Righteousness, rules there righteously over a justified people.

LXXVII.

WHITSUNTIDE.

"*Thus saith the Lord God, Come from the four winds, O breath, and breathe upon these slain, that they may live.*"—Ezekiel xxxvii. 9.

Introduction. Describe the vision of the dry bones.

Subject. This vision shows us the state of man before, and after, the Spirit of GOD has breathed.

1. The apostles before Pentecost, what were they? Timid, ignorant, feeble, helpless, dead and dry. Then the Spirit breathed on them, and lo! they are filled with zeal, they traverse the world preaching the Divinity of CHRIST, and the Resurrection from the Dead, and seal their mission with their lives.

2. So with the Church. What is she but an army of vivified men? The Spirit of GOD has breathed on the broken and scattered relics of humanity, dead in sin, dry and barren to good works, and lo! an army marches under the banner of the Cross, inspired with the Divine life.

3. So with you. Are you dead, and hard, and cold, barren and dry, and unprofitable? How many, O my GOD! are there who once lived to Thee, that are now dead and dry. Sin hath slain them, and they are impenetrable to the dews of Thy mercy. Dead to righteousness, dry to good.

"Come from the four winds, O Spirit, and breathe upon these slain, that they may live!"

Come from the East, O Breath of GOD, and breathe on the little ones whose life is dawning, in whom as yet is no response to Divine Love, fill them with piety and simplicity, fill them with that life which is hid with CHRIST in GOD, that they may live!

Come from the South, O Breath of GOD! and breathe on those who are in noon of life, in the sultry heat of temptations which surround them, lest they fall a prey to the robbers that lie in wait, and they be left naked and wounded in the way. Fill them with zeal, fill them with enthusiasm, fill them with the spirit of self-sacrifice, fill them with penitence when they have fallen, that they may live.

Come from the North, O Breath of GOD! and breathe on those on whom the snows have fallen. Breathe on those who are cold, and frozen, and hard, having resisted Thy inspirations heretofore, who are rigid in their obduracy, stiff in their unprofitableness:

> "Bend the stubborn heart and will,
> Melt the frozen, warm the chill,
> Guide the steps that go astray,"

ere it be too late, and thou ceasest to strive with them, that they may not die, but live.

Come from the West, O Breath of GOD! and breathe on those whose day is closing, whose sun sets, ere the night sinks down upon them, and endless darkness be their portion. O Spirit, breathe upon these slain, that they may live!

LXXVIII.

TRINITY SUNDAY.

"*And God said, Let us make man in our image, after our likeness.*"—Gen. i. 26.

Introduction. We have come now to the conclusion of the great drama of our LORD'S life and work. We have seen the FATHER sending the SON, and the SON coming into the world. We have seen the SON also leaving the world that He might ascend to the FATHER, and pour forth the HOLY GHOST upon men. We saw last Sunday the HOLY SPIRIT given; now the Church sums up all this history, and to-day directs us to recapitulate these mysteries, and show how perfectly they are united in one perfect scheme, and how it emanates from the Godhead, three in Persons, but one in Nature.

1. *The doctrine of the Trinity.* We believe that there are three Persons, but one GOD; that the FATHER is GOD, the SON is GOD, and the HOLY GHOST is GOD; and yet there are not three GODS, but one GOD; in the FATHER is manifested to man the Power, the SON, the Wisdom, and the SPIRIT, the Goodness of GOD.

2. *Exemplified in man.* Man was made in the image of God, and therefore we expect to see in him a reflection of this great mystery. And so we find it, imperfect however, because sin has troubled man's nature, so that the reflection is clouded and broken.

In man, however, the image is to be traced. Man is one, yet threefold; he has *Mind*, and *Body*, and *Soul*,—a Mind directing the Body, the Body executing the will of the Mind, and the Soul giving it life and energy.

Or look at the Mind alone, and see in that a triple stamp of its Creator; for in the mind are *Intelligence*, *Will*, and *Memory*,—Intelligence whereby man can understand about God, Will whereby he may seek Him, and Memory whereby he can recall His benefits. And these will be satisfied with God alone.

The Intelligence by the knowledge of God, the Will by coincidence with the Divine will, the Memory by the continuation of eternity.

3. *The effect of sin in marring the image.* But first must be healed the wounds of man wrought by sin. Man, by withdrawing from the Father, the Source of Power, has contracted *Infirmity*. By withdrawing from the Son, the Eternal Wisdom, he has contracted *Ignorance*. By withdrawing from the Holy Spirit, the Fountain of Goodness, he has contracted *evil concupiscence*.

Thus he has fallen under the power of three foes.

By Infirmity he has succumbed to the Flesh.

By Ignorance he has succumbed to the World.

By Concupiscence he has succumbed to the Devil.

And how can these wounds be healed?

By Faith his Ignorance can be enlightened.

By Hope his Infirmity may be overcome.

By Charity his Concupiscence may be counteracted.

4. *The recovery of the Image.* The work of our redemption is the restoration in us of the image which has been shattered by the Fall. To effect this, the whole Three Persons of the Trinity co-operate.

The FATHER helps us by drawing us to seek grace to recover what is lost.

The SON supplies us with grace through the Sacraments which He has instituted.

The HOLY SPIRIT keeps alive in us the Divine Life which is given us.

Conclusion. Inscrutable is the mystery of the Trinity. But we shall see all plain when the veil obscuring the Holy of holies is rent and drawn aside; then that which we have heard with the ear, we shall see with the eye. We shall behold the Ark of GOD's abiding Presence, the Rod of the Eternal FATHER's Power, the Tables of the SON's most perfect Wisdom, and the Manna of the SPIRIT's goodness.

Unto which blessed vision may GOD in His mercy bring us.

LXXIX.

CORPUS CHRISTI.

"*My beloved . . . . standeth behind our wall, he looketh forth at the windows, showing himself through the lattice.*"—Cant. ii. 9.

Introduction. The idea is that of a lover hiding from his mistress, who wanders in search of him. She says, "I will rise, and go about the city; in the streets, and in the broad ways, I will seek him whom my soul loveth."

All the while she searches, he is observing her with love, noting the trouble of her spirit, the tenderness which expresses itself in her tears.

Subject. *So Christ, hidden from us, observes us.*

1. Hidden in heaven He looketh forth at the windows, and beholds His Church in all her sorrow and tears, seeking Him whom her soul loveth, desolate without His Presence, weeping for His absence.

2. Hidden behind the wall of the Sacramental species, His eye is on us. Oh! how do we behave in that Presence? Where are our thoughts whilst our dear Lord is on the Altar? Then we should be seeking Him, straining the eye of our soul to see Him, extending our arms to hold Him fast, our whole hearts and souls absorbed in the contemplation of our Beloved.

He is there, hidden behind that wall, in His Godhead and His Manhood; He is there, our Beloved, without Whom we are desolate indeed.

3. Finally, He shows Himself at the lattice, and cries, "Rise up, My love, My fair one, and come away. For, lo, the winter is past, the rain is over and gone, the flowers appear on the earth, the time of the singing of birds is come, and the voice of the turtle is heard in our land. The fig tree putteth forth her green figs, and the vines with the tender grape give a good smell. Arise, my love, my fair one, and come away" (verses 11—13).

How glorious will be that time to the Church, when she recovers her Bridegroom, Who will comfort her heart and fulfil all her mind, Who will turn her mourning into laughter and her sorrow into joy.

How glorious also to each poor soul that has sought Him in fear and pain, that has yearned for Him, loving Him so dearly, and desiring His visible presence so greatly, to whom His Sacramental Presence has been the sun and life of her days on earth, but who has yearned for the full and unclouded vision of the Master and Bridegroom whom she loved and sought when hidden behind the wall of Sacraments.

Conclusion. What then is our lesson? 1. To seek JESUS through life, to seek Him with love and with tears, with love kindled by His love for us, with tears for our sins which hide Him from us.

2. To realise His Presence. Though hidden, He beholds us, His eye follows all our movements. Let us not forget to live as in His Presence.

LXXX.

MICHAELMAS.

"*Thousand thousands ministered unto Him, and ten thousand times ten thousand stood before Him.*"—Dan. vii. 10.

Introduction. The subject of this festival. A veil is drawn aside, and we are shown the order and harmony of the invisible world; we look to-day out of the material into the spiritual.

Subject. Let me this day lay before you the order of the heavenly host, and the work which they perform.

I. The angels are grouped into three orders—

1. Seraphim, Cherubim, Thrones } engaged in Adoration.

2. Dominions Principalities Powers	}	engaged in Strife with Evil.
3. Virtues Angel-guardians Archangels	}	engaged in the Custody of Creation.

All these offices are different, yet all angels are ministering spirits. Thus a seraph was sent to Isaiah, a cherub to guard Paradise, Michael, chief of Principalities, to Daniel, Raphael, a chief of virtues, to Tobias, and Gabriel, an archangel, to the Virgin Mary.

All in their ministry to GOD, minister to us men.

1. Angels are our guardians.
2. Archangels instruct us in the Divine Law.
3. Virtues attend to our health.
4. Powers drive far off the deadly foe.
5. Principalities govern our life aright.
6. Dominions strengthen us to control passion.
7. Thrones establish us in good begun.
8. Cherubim illumine with celestial wisdom.
9. Seraphim inflame with heavenly love.

Yet none of these orders of angels act independently of GOD, but GOD works mediately through them.

In Seraphim	it is	GOD Who	burns with love.
In Cherubim	,,	,,	enlightens with wisdom.
In Thrones	,,	,,	sits in equity.
In Dominions	,,	,,	reigns as Prince.
In Powers	,,	,,	excels in strength.
In Virtues	,,	,,	operates to heal.
In Archangels	,,	,,	beams as source of light.
In Angels	,,	,,	sends.

II. The offices of the angelic host are numerous.

1. Angels have charge over the elements. (Rev. vii. 1; xiv. 18; xvi. 1—10.)

2. Angels have guardianship over nations. (Dan. x. 13—20.)

3. Angels fight for us against Satan. (Rev. xii. 7.)

4. Angels guard us from peril. (Dan. vi. 22; iii. 28; Tobit xii.; Ps. xci. 11.)

5. Angels provide for the necessities of men. (Gen. xxi. 17; 1 Kings xix. 5, 6; Dan. xiv. 34—36.) As Hagar, Elijah, Daniel in the den.

6. Angels offer our prayers and good deeds before GOD. (Rev. viii. 3; Tobit xii. 12—15.)

7. Angels bear the souls of the departed to Paradise. (S. Luke xvi. 22.)

8. Angels have charge over the Catholic Church, they were guardians of the synagogue. (Rev. ii. 1, 8, 12, 18; iii. 1, 7, 14.)

9. Angels execute GOD's wrath. (Gen. xix. 1; Exod. xii. 23; 2 Kings xix. 35; Rev. xvi. 1.)

Conclusion. The Fathers taught that man was made to fill the void places vacated in heaven by the fall of Satan and his host. Thence the joy of the angels on the conversion of a sinner; thence the rage of the devils against man.

LXXXI.

ALL SAINTS.

"*Seeing we also are compassed about with so great a cloud of witnesses, let us lay aside every weight, and the sin which doth so easily beset us.*"—Heb. xii. 1.

Introduction. Describe a Roman amphitheatre and a Christian in the arena struggling with beasts. The witnesses by signs judged whether he had fought well or badly. In a gladiatorial fight the uplifted thumb gave sentence of life, the depressed thumb of death, to the gladiator who was down.

Subject. So are we encompassed by the Saints, who will be our judges.

Point I. *Who are the Saints?*

Men and women like ourselves, with no more grace than is or may be ours, with like temptations and passions. We are all called to be Saints, whether we will be or not depends on how we respond to our vocation.

Instance S. Genevieve, the little shepherdess, patron of Paris.

S. Cuthbert, the shepherd lad, patron of Durham.

S. Verena, the farm servant maid.

S. Isidore, the ploughman, patron of Madrid.

Point II. *What constitutes sanctity?*

Conquest over self. However much the saints may have differed from one another in other particulars, they all agreed in this one characteristic, they had obtained a mastery over themselves. They varied in other graces,—some were distinguished for their poverty of spirit, some for the spirit of penitence, some for their meekness, some for their hunger and thirst after righteousness, some were distinguished for their mercy, some for their purity, some as peacemakers, some for the cruel persecutions they endured,—but one and all, as the foundation of their sanctity, had acquired self-conquest.

Conclusion. Let us imitate these blessed ones by laying aside every weight, and our besetting sin, and let us run with patience the race that is set before us, looking unto JESUS, the author and finisher of our faith.

LXXXII.

THE COMMUNION OF SAINTS.

"*For I mean . . . . that now at this time your abundance may be a supply for their want, that their abundance also may be a supply for your want; that there may be equality: As it is written, He that had gathered much had nothing over; and he that had gathered little had no lack.*"—2 Cor. viii. 14, 15.

Introduction. Perhaps there is no article of the Creed to which attention has been so little directed in the Church of England as to that of the Communion of Saints. It is an article which has become practically to us a dead letter.

It has been thought, rightly or wrongly, that the Roman Church has gone into excess in her practical use of this article, but to use an article, even if that employment of it be excessive, is more pardonable than to bury it in the ground and make nothing of it.

Subject. The Communion of Saints.

Point I. By Communion we mean an interchange of loving offices, and union in holy things. As of old the faithful had all worldly goods in common, so now and ever they have all spiritual good things in common.

There is in the Church a communion of holy things. For we communicate in the same gifts of grace, the same Word of GOD and Gospel promises, the same faith and hope, and the same Sacraments, and are all partakers of the same Body of JESUS CHRIST.

There is not one faith for the wise and another for the poor, one hope for princes and another for paupers; but one Baptism, one Absolution, one Communion alike for all.

Point II. How is it in the world and social life? If one man is wealthy, a large circle profits by it, for his money is distributed amongst a number of tradesmen from whom he purchases. If one General gain a victory the whole nation reaps the advantage. If one man builds a magnificent monument, or lays out a park, numbers enjoy what he has done. So true is it that no man can live and die to himself alone. One man invented letters some thousands of years ago, and tens of thousands have profited by his discovery. One man discovered the power of steam about a century ago, and the whole of the civilized world is advantaged.

Very well, if, in ordinary life, the good deed of one man, or discovery of one man, becomes public property, and is to the profit of the community, so is it in the Church with regard to merit.

The good deeds of the Saints form a treasury of merit for the benefit of the Church.

As in a well-ordered house all share in the work and profit, so is it in the Church.

In a household the brother works abroad, the sister attends to the home—one brings money in, another lays it out on household affairs, and the work of each advantages the other, and the gain of each profits all. So is it in the Church. One reads and writes, another fasts, another prays, another gives alms, another suffers infirmities. Does each labour or endure for himself? By no means. You profit by my reading. I am advantaged by your prayers. One gives, and another receives his alms and is relieved; and the first profits by the example of the patience of him whom he relieves.

Conclusion. This is a great solace to the faithful. For if any one is detained through infirmity, or has no leisure for fasting or prayer, he may remember that though he cannot fast and pray, others are fasting and praying, and that he is a fellow-member with them. "I am a companion (partaker) of all them that fear Thee and keep Thy commandments." (Ps. cxix. 63.) By union of love and pious intention you partake in the good of others. If weak in body, think of the many religious in fasting, sackcloth, and ashes. If impeded in prayer, think of the prayers which ascend incessantly from the Universal Church. If unable to give alms, consider how many there are who give liberally, and by joining your intention to theirs, become a partaker of them; so that "their abundance may be a supply for your want."

LXXXIII.

THE GOVERNMENT OF THE HEART.

"*A good man out of the good treasure of the heart bringeth forth good things; and an evil man out of the evil treasure bringeth forth evil things.*" —S. Matth. xii. 35.

Introduction. The story of Tarpeia.

Point I. The citadel is the body of man. Tarpeia is the heart. Man is encompassed by the host of Satan. He knows that without is the enemy; but the heart does what the head would not do, enters into consultation with the enemy, and promises to admit the foe into the citadel, if she may be given that which is on the arm, meaning the bracelet of *pleasure in sin.* But when the foe enters she is overwhelmed with the bucklers, and sinks crushed under the *burden of sin.*

What is it we all ask when we admit the enemy? Is it not the pleasure? And what do we get? Is it not the burden?

Point II. *To Parents.*

Necessity of educating children in right principle, so as to be under the protection of principle, and not to be open to the treachery of feeling.

So that children may seek first to do what is right, rather than what they like.

1. Parents must act on principle themselves.

2. They must be careful to inculcate these principles.

Point III. *To the Young.*

Endeavour to make principle the rule of life. It will not fail and prove a Tarpeia.

Let the first question ever be—is such a thing right? Not—I should like such a thing, or I dislike such a thing. Likes and dislikes are the two hands of Tarpeia; she can throw open the door with either one; therefore let principle, not feeling, keep the key.

Do not tamper with conscience, so as to try and bend it to say what pleases the heart; that is making principle underling to feeling, putting Tarpeia above the Captain.

Conclusion. But if the heart be under control and made to do her work, you are perfectly safe. The heart is a very good servant in her proper place; but on no consideration allow her to keep the key of the Castle.

LXXXIV.

TRIFLING WITH CONSCIENCE.

"*And Balaam answered and said unto the messengers of Balak: If Balak would give me his house full of silver and gold, I cannot go beyond the word of the Lord my God, to do less or more. Now therefore I pray you, tarry ye also here this night, that I may know what the Lord will say unto me more.*"—Numb. xxii. 18, 19.

Introduction. The history of Balaam.

Subject. *Balaam is an instance of trifling with conscience.*

His wishes: "Let me die the death of the righteous, and let my last end be like his."

His profession: "If Balak would give me his house full of silver and gold, I cannot go beyond the word of the LORD my GOD, to do less or more."

His trifling: "Now tarry ye also here this night, that I may know what the LORD will say unto me more."

His end: Fighting against the very people whom GOD had made him bless.

Point I. *How the mischief began.*

That is tolerably clear. Balaam knew perfectly what GOD's will was; GOD had told him plainly enough; but when the honourable messengers made large promises, he began to think, Well, after all, GOD may have changed His Mind, or I may not have understood Him aright; I will inquire once again, and see if this second time He will answer more in accordance with my wishes and pecuniary advantage.

This history is a warning to us not to force conscience to speak as we please, to give a note that accords with our interest when he has sounded once a note of discord, has spoken once in words of reproof.

How often are we disposed to do this! When our wishes and our sense of what is right do not agree, we bend conscience to our wishes, not our wishes to conscience. We try to believe that that is right which we like, and to shut our eyes to seeing sin in what pleases us.

Examples.—A man has an opportunity of making unfair profit by another. He knows it is wrong, yet he argues with himself that he has himself been cheated, and that it is fair to recover what he has lost.

A child is urged by its wishes to some act of disobedience. It argues, I shall not be seen, the circumstances are not known. Perhaps my parent did not mean exactly this.

An opportunity of speaking truth which is unpleasant occurs. Evasion is sought, so as to deceive without telling an actual lie.

Point II. *Practical lessons.*

We may, I think, learn from the fall of Balaam these practical lessons :—

1. Beware of evading a plain duty.

2. Beware of allowing your pleasure to master your sense of right and wrong.

3. Beware of contracting a habit of arguing with conscience, and thus of deceiving your own soul.

LXXXV.

SLANDER.

"*And the people . . . . abode at Hazeroth.*"—Numb. xi. 31.

Introduction. The camp of Israel had gone on steadily from the Red Sea on its way towards the Promised Land, with the Pillar of the Cloud leading them by day; when all at once, to the surprise of every one, the Pillar of the Cloud stood still, and the journey of the Israelites was arrested at Hazeroth.

What was the cause? What stayed the people in their advance? I will tell you. Moses had married an Ethiopian woman, much to the annoyance of Aaron and Miriam, who went tittle-tattling up and down the camp about this match of Moses, saying many hard and nasty things, and some things that were not true.

Then the cloud stood still, and Miriam was smitten with leprosy.

Subject. *We learn from this the evil of gossip and slander.* It has two effects. (1.) It arrests the advance of the soul. (2.) It covers the soul with leprosy of evil.

Point I. *It arrests the advance of the soul.*

It is a sin so subtle and so easily committed, that people are guilty of it, and it grows to become a habit, before they are aware. The secret motive of detraction is self-love. People are envious of the good report of others, and they endeavour to lower others, so as to advance themselves. It is a great mistake, for they lower themselves by so doing. "Speak not evil one of another, brethren." The ancient Romans were given up of GOD because they were "full of envy, malignity, whisperers, backbiters." S. Paul warns the Corinthians lest there be among them "envyings, wrath, strife, backbitings."

All sin hinders the advance of the soul, and the sin of slander is not an exception to the rule. Just consider what notice GOD took of the evil-speaking of Aaron and Miriam. Because of this, the whole of that great host of Israelites was arrested in its march, and refused permission to go forward till it had been put away from among them.

Point II. *It covers the soul with leprosy.*

Yes, it is a sin so insidious, that in a little while it thoroughly demoralizes the whole nature, chokes spiritual growth, and makes the soul sick. It is a foul sin, unpleasant to all, one that makes all shun you. So-and-so is a gossip, is a backbiter; he or she is regarded with dislike, and no one has a good word to say for the gossip, because slander is a weapon against which no one is invulnerable, and therefore which all dread.

But when some spiteful, nasty story affecting a neighbour's character is over all the parish, and I go round and try to sift it to the bottom, and track it to its source, what do I hear at every cottage? Mrs. A. says, "Please, sir, I never invented it, Mrs. B. told me, and I merely repeated what I had heard." Mrs. B. says, "I heard it from Miss C., and I only said, I heard it was reported." Miss C. says her authority was Mr. D., and Mr. D. heard it from Mrs. E., and so on interminably. No one is answerable for the slander, but every one helps it on.

Now listen to me.

Nebuchadnezzar had a dream; he saw a great statue of gold and iron and brass and clay, reach up to the clouds. And he saw a little stone, "cut without hands out of the mountain," smite it, and down fell the goodly statue, a ruin.

So with many a slanderous tale—no one owns it, "it is not mine." Oh no! it is "cut without hands out of the mountain," but every one puts out a hand to give it a roll, and it strikes some fair character, and down it goes, and no one is responsible for the injury done.

Conclusion. When you hear a story affecting another person's character, before you retail it, pass it through three sieves.

1. Is it kind?
2. Is it true?
3. Is it necessary?

LXXXVI.

ON REFERRING ALL THINGS TO GOD.

"*Hezekiah received the letter of the hand of the messengers, and read it: and Hezekiah went up into the house of the Lord, and spread it before the Lord.*"—2 Kings xix. 14.

Introduction. Hezekiah, king of Judah, and Hoshea, king of Israel, had revolted against the king of Assyria.

Shalmanezar, king of Assyria, had gathered a mighty army, and had carried Israel away captive. And Sennacherib marched against Judah. What, was Hezekiah to resist him! Ten tribes were gone, how could two stand? One city after another fell, and at last Jerusalem was besieged. A haughty letter is sent to Hezekiah, defying his God; and the king takes the letter and spreads it before God.

Subject. *In all difficulties and affliction act as did Hezekiah.*

Point I. *In affliction.* When some great sorrow comes on you, do not repine. Job lost his seven sons and three daughters in one day, and what did he do? He took his grief and spread it before the Lord, and "the Lord blessed the latter end of Job more than his beginning." When loss of worldly goods comes, do not murmur. Job had flocks and herds taken from him; he spread his grief before the Lord, and "the Lord gave Job twice as much as he had before." Or when health fails, do not be angry. Job was sore afflicted in his body: he spread his grief before the Lord, "What, shall we receive good at the hand of God, and shall we not receive evil?" And in the end God healed him.

Point II. *In difficulties.* Sometimes these difficulties are the sore pressure of temptation. Without, the world strives to woo us, within, the heart is filled with evil desires; sometimes the struggle is beyond us, and we know not what to do. Go, dear soul, in thy sore trouble, and spread it before the Lord. Christ knows the weakness of the flesh. He took flesh to feel for man. Christ knows the allurements of the world, for Satan showed Him all its glory, in a moment, on the mount. Go, spread thy sorrow before Him, and show Him thy helplessness, and never fear, He will hear thee, strengthen thee, and succour thee.

Point III. *Where to spread one's troubles before the Lord.* It was into the house of the Lord that Hezekiah went to spread the letter. It was into the house of the Lord also that Hannah went when insulted and slandered by Peninnah : "Her adversary provoked her to make her fret," and she went into the house of God, and there in the bitterness of her soul she prayed and wept.

It is in God's house especially that we should seek to spread our grief before the Lord ; and especially when He is present on His Throne in the Blessed Sacrament.

I remember one evening in Switzerland finding a poor idiot woman, whom rude boys had been jeering and pelting with earth, in a church, kneeling before the Blessed Sacrament, telling her grief to her dear Lord amidst many sobs.

Let us learn to come before Him as did Hezekiah, Hannah, and that poor idiot, and spread our affliction before Him. Then with Hannah say : "I am of a sorrowful spirit : I have poured out my soul before the Lord ; out of the abundance of my complaint and grief have I spoken ;" and of a certainty the answer will come to us, which came to Hannah : "Go in peace : the God of Israel grant thee thy petition that thou hast asked of Him."

LXXXVII.

THE SUFFICIENCY OF GOD'S GRACE.

"*The barrel of meal shall not waste, neither shall the cruse of oil fail, until the day that the Lord sendeth rain upon the earth.*"—1 Kings xvii. 14.

Introduction. Narrate the circumstances.

Subject. *This has a mystical interpretation.*

Point I. The widow is the Gentile world; its nature, once good as it left God's hand, wasted, a handful of original goodness alone left, and but a few drops of Divine grace remaining. It despairs for its children. The religious systems of antiquity had failed to raise morality, and to give principle as a guide to life. The schemes of philosophy had also broken down—there was nothing to hinder the moral and social ruin of the world.

The Gentile world sent up its agonized cry for its children. It would consume its last remains of natural goodness, on the dry sticks of its faded system, and die, die, die!

Oh! think of the poor parents of heathen times with families of young boys and girls growing up, and no principle to give them upon which to bid them stand against the moral pollution which flooded the civilized world. Nothing to give those dear little ones to hold them up through life; nothing to give them to afford some hope that they would not rot like the rest of that decaying world. Poor parents, theirs was a bitter time!

Then, in that moment of despair, came Jesus; without the city He met the widowed world, and asked of her a little cake, a little of that humanity to take to Himself, that He might become very Man. He came to her as she gathered two sticks. On the two sticks of the Cross, that she had laid in order, He found her, and then He bade her eat and live and feed her sons.

Point II. "And the barrel of meal wasted not, neither did the cruse of oil fail, according to the word of the LORD, which He spake by Elijah." No! nor does it fail now.

For what is the meal but the true Bread that came down from Heaven, even CHRIST sacramentally our Food? And what is the oil but Divine grace given at Pentecost, and flowing ever in the channels of the Church?

They shall not fail—this Bread of Heaven and this celestial unction—till the rain, the latter rain, descend on the earth at the end of all things.

LXXXVIII.

REPARATION.

"*What reward shall I give unto the Lord for all the benefits that He hath done unto me?*"—Ps. cxvi. 11.

Introduction. If a man has done something and suffered for his country, his country seeks to make reparation for what he has suffered. A soldier loses an arm, he is given a pension. A general gains a battle, a statue is erected to him, and he is given a title. A politician carries a bill of great public utility through the House at great personal labour, and he is rewarded by a street or square being named after him. If any one has suffered for us, we do our utmost to recompense it. A servant is injured in the discharge of his or her duties; we do what we can to make it up to the servant.

Subject. *This principle of reparation underlies Christian worship.* What has not CHRIST suffered for us? Consider His Poverty, His Persecution, His Passion.

How do we seek to make reparation? I answer: Every cathedral and church is a reparation to Him who, for our sakes, had not where to lay His Head. Every hymn and psalm sweetly sung is an act of reparation for the cries of "Crucify Him! crucify Him!"

Why do we deck our altars with flowers and velvet and gold? Because the soldiers gave Him thorns, and stripped Him of His garments.

Why do we offer our bowed knees and bended heads? Because the soldiers mocked Him with their bowed knees, and the Jews shook their heads in scorn at Him.

Objection I. But, you object, CHRIST when on earth was poor and lowly; therefore surely a poor and bare church and service befits Him now.

I beg your pardon. Three wise men came from the East to worship Him. They found Him in rags on the knee of a poor woman, in a cave which served as a stable. Now had these three Magi been of your opinion, they would have said: "Surely He loves Protestant simplicity, mean clothing, poverty, and nakedness—we will pack up again our treasures, keep them for ourselves, and worship Him, sitting down on that log of wood, with our hats on our heads, in spirit only."

But the Magi acted the very reverse—they fell down before that poor little Baby lapped in rags, and opening their caskets, poured forth their treasures, gold and frankincense and myrrh.

I suspect those who argue so eagerly for Protestant simplicity really mean this : Let us keep all the good things for ourselves, and let GOD have the scraps.

Objection II. But, you object, all we can give, the best, is nothing to GOD.

Quite so: but GOD asks them as a token of affection, and values them as an evidence that we are ready to give Him what we can, because we love Him.

A little child brings its mother a bunch of withered forget-me-nots; the little bunch is not worth a farthing, but she treasures the little cluster.

A son in Australia gets a photograph from home. He sets it in a gold frame over his chimney-piece, and yet it cost his parents sixpence! Does he value it at sixpence? No, he loves it because it proves to him that the memory of their son is still warm in the hearts of the old folks at home.

Conclusion. The principle of making a return is natural. If we make none we are ungrateful. To make a return is a law of nature : the field is given dressing, and returns a good crop; the sea receives the rivers, and returns the clouds : give a hyacinth bulb water, and it returns a flower. GOD gives abundantly, let us not return stingily. GOD gives gladly, let us not return grudgingly, for GOD loveth a cheerful giver.

LXXXIX.

PREJUDICES.

"*We know in part . . . . but when that which is perfect is come, then that which is in part shall be done away.*"—1 Cor. xiii. 9, 10.

Introduction. GOD alone knows all things perfectly, and we must be content to know in part. Some may know more than others, but none know all things.

A farmer knows about agriculture, a sailor about navigation, a mechanic about engines, a botanist about herbs, a geologist about stones, an astronomer about stars. A very knowing man may be at one and the same time a good agriculturist, sailor, mechanic, botanist, geologist and astronomer, but there are a host of other things of which he knows nothing.

A farmer is a fool if he dogmatizes on navigation, a mechanic if he lays down the law upon stars.

Subject. *It is the same with religious truth*—we know but in part.

Point I. There is much, very much in GOD's truth which we do not know. We must be content that so it should be. If a sailor abuses the science of agriculture, or a farmer the art of navigation, you say he is a prejudiced person, and that is only an elegant way of saying that he is ignorant, and too conceited to know his ignorance.

Very well. In religion there are heaps of people who lay down the law on things they know nothing about, and deny doctrines and truths of which they have not a glimmer of understanding. They say, I don't believe in this or that, and therefore what I don't believe in is false.

Such persons are ignorant and prejudiced; they do not know that the horizon of the man on the top of a mountain is wider than that of the man buried up to his neck in the earth.

Point II. Now you will see in what heresy consists. Heresy is in fact the denial of truths we know not, or do not understand. Heresy is not the teaching of anything definite, it is the denial of definite truths taught by the Church.

What are all the heresies of ancient and modern times?

The Gnostics denied the Humanity of CHRIST.

The Arians denied the Divinity of CHRIST.

The Pelagians denied the efficacy of grace.

The Calvinists deny the freedom of the will.

The Lutherans deny moral responsibility.

The Presbyterians deny the Divine authority of the Episcopate.

The Congregationalists deny the Divine constitution of the Church.

The Baptists deny the efficacy of infant baptism.

The Quakers deny all sacramental efficacy whatever.

Heresy is therefore denial of truths. Protestantism is a system of prejudice or denial, denial of the Eucharistic Presence and Sacrifice, of the Communion of Saints, Purgatory, and the like. It is simply a system of disbelief, or a carrying of ignorance into religion, and exalting ignorance into a criterion of truth.

Conclusion. Now put away prejudice, whether in secular matters or in religious matters; for prejudice is only conceited ignorance. Try to have a humble spirit, and learn that all you know, and can know, is partial. The Jews had a veil on their hearts, cast there by pride and prejudice, which so obscured their vision that they protested against and denied JESUS CHRIST when He stood amongst them. So the Catholic Truth stands amongst us, and the veil is on our hearts, and we repudiate the truth because we are too blind to see it, and too conceited to try to see it.

Confess the possibility of there being other food than milk for babes in religion, and so go on in faith to perfection.

XC.

TRUE DEVOTION.

"*Pour out thine heart like water before the face of the Lord; lift up thy hands towards Him.*"—Lam. ii. 19.

Introduction. Where there is love there is true devotion. Look at a loving wife's thought for her husband, or a mother's for her child; how her mind is incessantly occupied with the object of her love, and how she revolves every means she can of affording pleasure to the object of her solicitude, how she grieves at any cloud obscuring the familiarity of their intercourse, any separation which interferes with the frequency of their converse.

Subject. Such is true devotion, when the object of love is GOD.

Point I. *False Devotion.*

Now people are very apt to deceive themselves and suppose themselves to be devout when they are nothing of the sort. When Saul's emissaries came to seize David, Michal put a bolster in his bed and let David escape. So we put bolsters in the place of David too often in all our religious matters.

One is given to much frequenting of Church, is there for

Matins and Evensong, communicates once or twice a week, and reads devotional books, yet her heart all the while is full of rancour against a neighbour—there's a bolster instead of David.

Another mortifies and denies himself food and sleep, and is assiduous in bridling his animal nature, but takes no little pride in his austerities, and flatters himself he is becoming a saint—there's another bolster instead of David.

Another again is liberal in charities, gives readily to the poor, to missions, to the building and adornment of churches, but is chary of forgiveness to one who has wronged him—there also is a bolster in place of David.

Point II. *True Devotion.*

True devotion consists in an eminent degree in love, which makes us prompt, active, and diligent in the observance of GOD's commandments. He who loves, grieves to offend the person loved.

Love seeks the society of the loved one, love is ready to make sacrifice for the benefit of the person beloved.

That is not true love which fails in one of these particulars. So that is not true devotion which consists in frequent worship, but little heed whether we offend GOD. Nor is that true devotion which consists in sacrifice, but indifference to the society of GOD in prayer.

True devotion is not acquired all at once, but by little and little it grows, and as it grows it exhibits the three characteristics I have mentioned—

1. Contrition, i.e., grief at offending GOD.
2. Love of prayer, i.e., delight in converse with GOD.
3. Self-sacrifice, i.e., love of suffering for GOD.

Pure white light is made up of three coloured rays—red, blue, and yellow. Substract one of the constituents, and you get a dingy, dirty ray. So devotion is only pure and perfect when marked with these three characteristics.

Conclusion. How true devotion may be obtained.

1. By acquiring a love of GOD and a hatred of sin.
2. By constant recollection, or abiding in the presence of GOD.
3. By oblation of all we do and all we suffer to Him.
4. By frequent and exact purification of conscience.
5. By frequent communion.

XCI.

THE CASTING OF THE VESSELS.

"*All the vessels which Hiram made to king Solomon for the house of the Lord were of bright brass. In the plain of Jordan did the king cast them, in the clay ground between Succoth and Zarthan.*"—1 Kings vii. 45, 46.

Introduction. There was a plain of barren land, with here and there upon it a stagnant pool, between Succoth and Zarthan. The shepherd pitched not his tent there, the grass was scanty and rank, and he said, This land is vile and worthless. The peasant ran not his plough through it; the clay was too stiff to be worked profitably, and he said, This land is valueless and to be despised.

Times passed, and that land still lay bare and neglected. Then Solomon cast his eye about for a place where he might form the vessels of bright brass for the Sanctuary of the LORD, and it fell on this clay ground between Succoth and Zarthan.

Subject. *So it is with the casting of the vessels for the House of God above.*

Point I. What a sad history is that of the poor before CHRIST's coming, if indeed they can be said to have had a history. They were slaves, serfs, despised; no man regarded them, thought of their feelings, supposed they were capable of anything good. The great men of the world, princes, and nobles, and landlords, they had a history: but the poor!—here and there in history we come upon a great patch of blood, now and then a piercing cry of woe, feeble hands stretched out in agony—that is all their history, till the Carpenter's Son came and healed the broken-hearted, and preached deliverance to the captives, and chose the mean clay ground in which to mould the first pillars of His Church. In the Carpenter's shop of Nazareth He formed S. James, among the fishing-nets, by the sea of Tiberias, He shaped S. Peter and S. John, at the custom-table of the despised tax-collector He cast that vessel of bright brass, S. Matthew, for His new and glorious Temple.

So was it in the first age of the Church, out of the clay ground of poverty and slavery rose the first vessels for the Sanctuary.

Point II. And now we know that there is no rank or station, however low, however despised, upon which the eye of the great Master Builder does not fall, and which He does not accept, in it to fashion His saints, pillars for His Temple, vessels for His Sanctuary.

On a certain summer's day, if you were to visit Madrid, the capital of Spain, you would see flags flying, you would hear the bells of all the churches ringing, processions sweeping through the streets with banner, and hymn, and band. You would see crowds in holiday attire hastening to the churches, and all keeping high festival. Why all this rejoicing? The capital of this great nation is keeping the feast of its patron. And who is this patron?—a king, a bishop, a noble, a great theologian? Oh, no! only a poor ploughman, S. Isidore.

Look along the hedges in early summer and see how blue they are with speed-well. What is the name given this lovely flower in Italy, and Spain, and France? This flower so dear to the dweller in the country, because, so frail and delicate, it throws so exquisite a beauty over our hedgerows, is called Veroniça, after a poor farm girl near Milan, whose virtues have made her worthy to be numbered with the Saints.

And let this be to you an encouragement. "Hath not God chosen the poor, rich in faith?" asks S. James.

Point III. Now we are very apt to say, "Ah! if God had put us in some different position from that in which we actually are, we could serve Him better!" What! you want to pick and choose your soil, in which to be cast. Believe me, God knows best what sort of soil is most suited for casting His vessels of bright brass. It is not in light crumbly garden earth, but in stiff clay, that this must be done.

You are a farmer. "Ah! if it were not that I had to occupy my attention so much with things of the farm, with looking after the men, who try my temper, &c." Why! this is the clay soil, my friend.

You are a mother. "Ah! if it were not for those squalling children, pulling at me all day long, their clothes to wash and mend, their meals to cook; they leave me no time for thinking of my soul, for prayer and meditation." Why! here is clay ground, my friend.

You are a servant. "Ah! I have to dance attendance

on my mistress, to put up with her whims, to be called to account for nothing. There are my fellow-servants always enticing me into what is wrong, so many occasions when I must tell lies." Clay ground again.

Who put you in this position, I ask? Did not the hands of CHRIST place you there? Does He not know your temptations, your difficulties, all the impediments in your way? To be sure He does. Therefore be not discouraged, use that clay ground, despise it not, and in it He will mould you for His holy Temple, eternal in the heavens.

XCII.

FREE-WILL.

"*Not by constraint, but willingly and of a ready mind.*"—1 S. Pet. v. 2.

Introduction. When GOD made man, it was in His image, i.e., with the plenitude of being. And the plenitude of being consists in the possession of a free-will, their course is marked out for them, and they must traverse it. The oscillation of the animal will is greater than that of the vegetable, and that is all.

By giving man a free-will, GOD has placed man in a different relation to Him, from that of the beast. To the beast GOD is a ruler who rules by compulsion. The water must run down hill, the plant must thrust upwards, the insect must traverse its stages of larva and imago, the beast must obey its instinct, and each acts a part predetermined for it, and has no idea of the possibility of independent action, of running beyond its groove.

But GOD by giving man a free-will liberates man from the law of compulsion, and makes his obedience an act of free-will. GOD does not constrain, but persuade; man does not obey because he must, but because he ought.

Point I. GOD gives man certain faculties to use or to abuse, according to the determination of his own free-will, to educate them or to obliterate them, to perfect or to spoil.

The oyster is born with embryo eyes, but as it never uses them in the sludge at the river bottom, it reabsorbs them, and they are found only in an undeveloped condition in the mature fish. So we are born with power, an intellect to be sharpened, feelings to be directed, a will to be regulated, a sense of the beautiful to be matured, a desire to know to be cultivated. Take care lest they share the fate of the oyster's eyes.

Have you not often noticed these rudimentary faculties in the child, and when it has grown up they have disappeared. I have observed the love a child has for flowers—it is the rudimentary sense of the lovely; the child grows up and becomes a farmer, and never notices flowers any more, the beautiful no longer affects his feelings, because, for want of cultivation, it has been reabsorbed like the eyes of the oyster.

Point II. So GOD gives us gifts of grace, appeals to conscience. There is no compulsion. He offers, we can accept or refuse as we will. The story is told in the life of a saintly woman, (Sœur Marie of Liége,) that she was present at the execution of an impenitent murderer, and she saw in vision above him a large cloud illumined with golden sun-light, swollen with blessings and ready to burst in love upon him, waiting only for his uplifted hand in prayer, for one expression of *desire* for forgiveness. But none was formed, and the cloud of blessings rolled away.

We have all that we can desire, all that is necessary for us offered. The wells of salvation overflow, if only we will draw from them—pardon for the guilty soul, healing for the sick, strength for the feeble, refreshment for the weary; but we must by an act of free-will seek the sources whence these flow, or God cannot give them us; for, to force on man what he is reluctant to receive, is to reverse His mode of dealings with man.

Point III. In those who are finally lost, the will is resolutely confirmed in its opposition to God. Where there is a will to amend, there there is the grace of God ready to meet it half-way, and confer power of amendment. But when the will has persistently refused the use of certain means, it acquires a hatred of them; when it has opposed a certain course of conduct, it acquires a hatred of it. Thus where prayer has been constantly neglected, there arises a dislike to it; where study has been refused, the acquisition of knowledge becomes odious; where goodness has been opposed, at first a positive dislike and then an abhorrence of virtue accrue.

Thus with the lost, having through life wilfully resisted the Will of God, they wilfully persist in resistance, because the distaste for sanctification, which is the Will of God, intensifies through eternity. They may envy the Blessed, but have no will to be like them, just as now, in life, the wicked man will sometimes be envious of the good man, but have no wish to be himself virtuous.

Conclusion. Remember then that the work of life is voluntary obedience to the Will of God, which Will desires our sanctification, and sanctification is the necessary quality disposing to enjoy eternal happiness.

XCIII.

OUR CHRISTIAN CALLING.

"*Walk worthy of the vocation wherewith ye are called.*"—Eph. iv. 1.

Introduction. We are taught by S. Paul that we have a vocation, or calling, and he requires us to walk worthy of it.

Point I. Our vocation is a Christian calling; we are called Christians after CHRIST. As the oil flowing from Aaron's beard went down to the skirts of his clothing, so the name of CHRIST descends to the smallest, and meanest and poorest, of His members united to Him by holy Baptism.

Our vocation is to live and to die to CHRIST—to take CHRIST as our pattern, and work out in ourselves His image.

Seneca when in prison was deprived of all his possessions, which were confiscated; so he bequeathed to his disciples all that remained to him—the example of his life.

So we have the example of CHRIST'S life as our perfect pattern, and as the inheritance of every disciple of CHRIST; and our work here is to study it and conform our lives to it.

Have you ever noticed a printer correcting a proof? He sets before him the copy, and goes over his work, and here is a wrong letter; he pulls it out and puts in a right one. Here is a letter reversed, he extracts it, and places it aright. And at last he has conformed his type to the copy before him. So must you deal with your lives. Set before you the Copy and go over your acts, and words, and thoughts, and rectify them by the Copy which is perfect.

Point II. But all who bear the name of Christian are not true Christians.

Of many it may be said, in the words of Revelation, (iii. 6,) "Thou hast a name that thou livest and art dead."

"They are not all Israel, which are of Israel, neither because they are the seed of Abraham are they all children." (Rom. ix. 7.)

It was the custom among the ancient Romans for noble children to bear on their breasts a golden bulla, impressed with the image of their father; and it was a matter of pride for a son to bear the honoured token on his bosom, and show that he was of a great house, and the son of a great man. The younger Scipio having disgraced himself, the Senate decreed that his bulla should be taken from him, as he was unworthy to bear his father's image and name.

So every Christian bears the name of his Lord, and His image impressed on his heart; but oh! if he disgrace that name and defile that image. Shall not both be taken away at that great and terrible day when the Lord comes with His saints to judge the world?

Conclusion. But the Apostle warns us, "Fight the good fight of faith, lay hold on eternal life; whereunto thou art also called." (1 Tim. vi. 12.) Called in baptism as soldiers are enrolled, and called to what? not apparently to fight as the end of our calling, but called to eternal life; and the fighting is only a transient passage, an accident of our calling.

XCIV.

THE BED OF DARKNESS.

"*I have made my bed in the darkness.*"—Job xvii. 13.

Introduction. What can be more sad than those terrible words of despondency uttered by Job, when he had lost all his possessions, and his health; and his friends had turned against him, and his righteousness in which he had prided himself turned to filthy rags.

"My days are past, my purposes are broken off, even the thoughts of my heart. They change the night into day; the light is short because of darkness. If I wait, the grave is mine house; I have made my bed in the darkness. I have said to corruption, Thou art my father: to the worm, Thou art my mother and my sister. And where is now my hope? As for my hope, who shall see it?"

Subject. These words said in a moment of profound depression by Job, and untrue for him, are yet terribly true for others.

Point I. Terribly true will these words be to him who has spent his life without making eternity his aim, whose days are past, and his purposes, all of this world, are broken off. "I will pull down my barns, and build greater," said the rich fool; "Soul, soul, thou hast much goods laid up for many years, take thine ease, eat, drink, and be merry." Then came GOD's message, "This night thy soul shall be required of thee!" Then might he exclaim in despair and truth, "My days are past, my purposes are broken off, even the thoughts of my heart."

How true also of one whose mind is occupied exclusively by business, whose purposes are business, the thoughts of whose heart are business only. Business is excellent, but not so when all-engrossing. There is a time for everything, enough also of everything. When these purposes are broken off, these thoughts of the heart, schemes which change night into day, as he tosses sleepless planning on his bed—when they come to an end, and there opens a void future, for which no preparation has been made, no thought taken, oh, well may that man cry out in despair, "I have made my bed in the darkness, and where is now my hope? As for my hope, who shall see it?"

A servant is given a candle, by the light of which he is to make, and get into, his bed. He wastes his time chattering in the kitchen or on the stairs, and then hurries to his room, and finds his candle flickering in its socket, and it expires ere he has made his bed. Then he has to make it in the dark. And a bed so made will probably prove a very uncomfortable couch for the night.

We are given the taper of life, by which we are to prepare our future bed, by the light of which we are to make ready for the place of our repose. How do we spend the time? Do we waste it, or do we use it? If we have employed our time otherwise, shall we find rest on that ill-made couch? I trow not, we have made our bed in the darkness.

Point II. Our LORD speaks of laying up treasure in heaven, as though it were possible to lay up there, whilst we are here on earth, a store of happiness which we shall reap after death.

We have a work to do here, a task set us, a duty to accomplish, and if it be not done, then we shall find we have made our bed in the darkness.

God did not send us here to dawdle through life, to wake in the morning, breakfast, potter about till lunch, drowse through the afternoon till dinner-time, and then talk empty nothings till tea and bed. Every day brings with it responsibilities. Every day something must be done, done for our own souls, or for the souls of others, or for the Church of God.

We are sent into the world to glorify God and save our own souls; and every morning we should resolve to do what we can, nay more, do something definite and practical, which, in the evening we can point to, as something effected towards one or other of these ends.

Solomon says of the virtuous woman, "She layeth her hands to the spindle." Do you know what the spindle is? It is that on which the flax spun off the distaff is wound when done. On the distaff is what she has to do, on the spindle is what she has done. See, he does not praise her for the amount of work she undertakes, but the amount she accomplishes.

Well, it is work done, and not work to be done, that we should look to with confidence, and which will deserve commendation of God. Look to thy distaff. How much hast thou to do? Look to thy spindle. How much hast thou done?

Look to what God has set thee to do—see how much of it thou hast accomplished. Injuries forgiven, not to be forgiven; restitution made, not to be made; pardon asked, not to be asked; confession made, not to be made; responsibilities executed, not merely undertaken.

XCV.

HOW MEN TREAT THEIR SOULS.

"Then Jacob was greatly afraid and distressed: and he divided the people that was with him, and the flocks, and herds, and the camels, into two bands: and said, If Esau come to the one company, and smite it, then the other company which is left shall escape. And Jacob lifted up his eyes, and looked, and behold, Esau came, and with him four hundred men. And he divided the children unto Leah, and unto Rachel, and unto the two handmaids. And he put the handmaids and their children foremost, and Leah and her children after, and Rachel and Joseph hindermost."—Gen. xxxii. 7, 8; xxxiii. 1, 2.

Introduction. The sagacity and nice judgment of Jacob are to be commended. He saw that there was great danger to be apprehended from his brother whom he had sorely wronged, and who came to meet him with four hundred armed men. What did Jacob then? He arranged his caravan in a sort of procession, graduated from what he held cheapest, which he put in the van, to what he held dearest, which he put in the rear. First went his sheep, then his oxen, then his camels; then came his servant-maids with their children, then Leah the wife he cared little for, with her children, and then last, furthest removed from danger, the dearly loved Rachel and her child Joseph, hindermost of all.

Subject. Men treat their souls in a manner exactly the reverse of Jacob, and therefore exhibit the extremity of indiscretion.

Point I. *The value of the soul.*

What is more precious than the soul? It is the breath

of God, an inspiration of the Divine nature—it is eternal. Christ died to redeem our souls—what shall a man give in exchange for his soul?

Weigh well its costliness. Our bodies are made of earth; God formed them of the clay, but He breathed into the nostrils of Adam the breath of life, and man became a living soul. It is the soul which raises us above the brute creation. The lion is stronger, the tiger more agile, the gazelle more beautiful, the horse swifter than man, but man, the feeble naked child, is greater and nobler than the noblest and greatest of the beasts, for he has a living soul, a spark of Divine fire.

Weigh well also what Christ suffered, to purchase our souls from the bondage into which they had fallen; how He laboured and suffered all to win the love, and winning the love, to break the chains of those poor souls which lay in darkness, and were fast bound in misery and irons.

Point II. *How we appreciate the soul.*

Now how do we treat our souls? If we valued them aright, we would venture everything, ere we risked them. We would send forth our caravan, as did Jacob, with our worldly prospects and home affections before our soul, which is most costly of all. But not so. We put the soul forward into every place of danger, let the soul run all the risks, and keep the worldly prospects, and worldly goods and affections in the rear.

Is such and such a transaction advantageous, such a connexion beneficial, such an association promising from a lucrative point of view? These are the considerations which actuate us, and we risk our souls that we may secure our goods.

Conclusion. Las Casas mentions an incident of his

Indian travel as follows: A Spaniard played a violin to a crowd of natives. One of the savages was so enchanted, that he begged to be allowed to try the violin himself. The Spaniard refused. Then the Indian threw himself down before him and said, "Let me but handle that instrument, and I give up myself, my wife, and children to be your slaves in perpetuity."

Do we not sometimes act thus? sell our future for some foolish, transitory pleasure?

XCVI.

THE CONTEMPLATION OF HEAVEN.

"*I reckon that the sufferings of this present time are not worthy to be compared with the glory that shall be revealed in us.*"—Rom. viii. 18.

Introduction. It is a good thing to fix for awhile our eyes on eternal happiness.

Swimming my horse across a broad river in Iceland, and made giddy by the whirling stream, my guide cried to me, "Look to the shore! By keeping the eye fixed thereon the giddiness passes."

I bid you now do the same. The whirl of life is about you, time rushes past, the wave of trouble rises against you —Look to the shore.

Subject. *Suffering now—glory hereafter*, this is what the Apostle speaks of.

Point I. Cleopas and another disciple on Easter Day in the evening, were going to Emmaus, and they talked together sadly of CHRIST's sufferings. They recalled His stripes and buffetings, the mockery, the crown of thorns, the purple robe, the reed, the nails, the spear. Then came Jesus and walked by their side, and their eyes discerned Him not. Then He said, "What manner of communications are these that ye have one with another, as ye walk and are sad?" And when they told Him that they spake of the Passion, the sufferings of Christ, those sad things that had taken place, He asked, "*What things?*" as though He knew not, or remembered not, what had taken place.

For the joy set before Him, He had endured the Cross, despising the shame, and now that He was risen, He counted not those sorrows and pains. "What things?"—they were nothing to His Resurrection joy.

So will it be with the Blessed. Speak to them of the things they endured here below—the contradiction of sinners, the evil report, envy, insult, wrongs they underwent. "What things? Oh, we remember them no more in our present joy." Speak to the martyrs of their cruel torments, the axe, the rack, the stake, the saw, the cross, the leaded whip, the wild beasts wherewith they fought. "What things? Oh, they were nothing, they have faded like a dream in our present gladness."

Ah! you might speak now to S. Paul of his labours more abundant, his stripes above measure, his frequent prisons, his stoning, his three shipwrecks, the night and day in the deep; his journeyings often, his perils of water, perils of robbers, perils of his own countrymen, perils by the heathen, perils in the city, perils in the wilderness, perils on the sea, perils among false brethren; his weariness and painfulness, his watchings often, his hunger, and thirst, and fastings often, his cold and nakedness. Oh! what a list to remember! "What things?"

Point II. The glory is to be revealed in us—in our own selves. These poor mean bodies of ours, these feeble, timorous souls will be the chosen vessels for the revelation of future glory. The soul will have struggled through its encumbrances, will have had purged away in the fire that tries every man's work, its dross, that dross that all saw here, so that few marked the sterling metal, and it will shine forth in its full power, growing in knowledge and love through eternity. The soul delights in knowing and it delights in loving; GOD is infinite, and through eternity it will be acquiring fresh knowledge of the infinite perfections of GOD and His works, and will be acquiring more love for Him whom it knows ever more perfectly. And the body raised and glorified will ever be in the presence of the glorious GOD-Man.

XCVII.

THE WARFARE OF LIFE.

"*Is there not a warfare* (margin) *to man upon earth?*"—Job vii. 1.

Introduction. Job speaks the truth, there is a warfare for man, one that lasts through his life. A warfare waged against Satan, but not against him only, but also against Self.

Point I. Now I wish you to observe what Job says in another passage, and how he made that Self which might have been his adversary into an auxiliary in the war. He says (Job xxxi. 1), "*I made a covenant with mine eyes.*"

Would you know what this covenant means? I take it this is its signification, and it was contracted on these terms.

"My Eyes! you shall not gaze on harmful sights, I will turn away mine eyes from beholding vanity. You shall be under restraint for a few years, but at the Resurrection you shall see the King in His beauty. I have made a covenant with mine eyes.

"My Feet! you shall not walk in the way of sinners, nor tread the paths of death. You shall walk in the narrow road, along the traces left by CHRIST, Who went before dragging His Cross. This for a while; but, at the Resurrection, you shall walk the streets of Jerusalem and tread the gardens of Paradise. I have made a covenant with my feet.

"My Hands! you shall not deal unjustly, nor work wickedness, but shall labour diligently to execute what is laid upon you by GOD. You shall be lifted up in prayer, and be stretched out in almsgiving to the poor. And at the Resurrection Day you shall clasp Him Who is the Word of Life you handled, once hidden in the Eucharistic species, now in unveiled Majesty. I have made a covenant with my hands.

"My Lips! you shall speak no guile; slanderous speeches, and untruth, and hard words shall not be uttered by you. I will control you that you speak discreetly, and hereafter you shall sing without wearying the praises of CHRIST, and kiss His Sacred Wounds. I have made a covenant with my lips."

Now this is a course I commend to you. Enlist the body in the work of warfare, make a covenant with it, and keep it to the terms of its agreement, by a resolute will strengthened by the Grace of GOD.

Point II. And only think of the happiness when the war is over and victory is won.

"To him that overcometh will I give the hidden manna." (Rev. ii. 17.) Manna signifies, What is this? and this is the meaning here. To him that overcometh, saith CHRIST, will I give that which is indescribable, which eye hath not seen, nor ear heard, neither hath it entered into the heart of man to conceive.

Oh! the Blessed will exclaim when they receive their reward, It is manna! What is this? For a cup of cold water given in the name of a disciple, so great a gift!

Oh! it is manna! What is this? For a little struggle against a besetting sin, so many falls and so few conquests, yet the warfare continued in spite of discouragement, so great and glorious a crown!

Oh! it is manna! What is this? This for having given up my little comforts, that I might dedicate of my superfluity to the service of GOD. I gave a few pence a week, and this in reward—this manna!

Oh! it is manna! For attending lovingly on the sick, in spite of the disgust and unpleasantness accompanying sickness, what is this so great a repayment!

Oh! it is manna! A little hour on Sundays given up to the instruction of children in the Faith, and their religious duties, and all this reward? What is this, my GOD?

"I reckon that the sufferings of this present time are not worthy to be compared with the glory that shall be revealed in us." (Rom. viii. 18.)

XCVIII.

REUNION.

"*And he fell upon his brother Benjamin's neck, and wept; and Benjamin wept upon his neck. Moreover, he kissed all his brethren, and wept upon them: and after that, his brethren talked with him.*"—Gen. xlv. 14, 15.

Introduction. I know of few more moving passages in Scripture than the account of the reunion of Joseph and his brethren. The tears and joy on all sides, old quarrels and envy and injuries forgotten in the sweetness of seeing dear old faces once more, and hearing once more old familiar voices, and talking once more of old home.

Subject. *Such a meeting will be ours hereafter.* Let us consider for a while the blessedness of the meeting on the Resurrection morning.

Point I. *The meeting with those we have benefited here.*

Teachers, parents, think of that! Think that possibly some glad one, on that day, may come to you and say, "After God it is to you that I owe it that I am here now. You taught me the Truth, you taught me my duty." And may be, wondrous will be the surprise of some humble soul, to find herself surrounded by many who will greet her with love as one whose example had upheld them in the struggle of life.

Point II. *The meeting of friends and relations.*

The child and its mother, the husband and the wife, the brother and sister. Oh! the overflowing hearts, and eyes moist with happy tears! Oh! the outstretched arms, and hearts beating with gladness to see the grave return those committed to it in faith and hope, restored to be companions through eternity!

The making up of friendships which have been broken.

The difference of the parting and the meeting.

The deathbed of the mother—aged, and worn with sickness.

The resurrection of the mother in the bloom of youth and beauty.

Point III. *The meeting with Mary and the Saints.*

Think of the rapture of seeing her who bore JESUS, from whom He drew the Blood which redeemed us, the Body which nourished us; her whom He loved so dearly, her whom He assumed to Heaven and crowned queen of angels?

Think of the meeting with the Saints, with S. Vincent of Paul, S. Benedict, S. Dominic, S. Francis, S. Lawrence, S. Agnes, S. Margaret, S. Sebastian, with the Apostles, with S. Peter and S. John; with the fathers of the old covenant; of conversing familiarly with Moses and David, and Abraham and Adam.

Point IV. *The meeting with Jesus.*

This will be the chiefest joy of all, to see Him whom we have loved above all others; our chiefest, best beloved; to see that dear Face so full of love, to touch the five venerable wounds, to look into those compassionate eyes.

I was once in a railway carriage with a mother and her baby. The little thing was asleep, but it woke and looked in alarm from face to face, and saw all strange; then the features quivered, and the eyes filled with tears; but all at once it looked up and saw the mother's countenance. Instantly the child was as though transfigured. Away fled every trace of fear and distress, out flew the little arms, and in an instant it had clasped its mother's neck and had buried its smiling face in her cheek.

I thought at the moment of our resurrection. We shall see strange faces around us, all will be new and startling—but when our eyes rest on Him and see the wounds, we shall be at rest, in joy—away, away with all fear! "I know that, when He shall appear, I shall be like Him; for I shall see Him as He is." (1 S. John iii. 2.)

XCIX.

DESIRE TO SEE JESUS.

"*Sir, we would see Jesus.*"—S. John xii. 21.

Introduction. There were certain Greeks amongst those who came to Jerusalem to worship at the feast; these came to Philip and desired him, saying, "Sir, we would see Jesus." Philip told Andrew, and Andrew and Philip together told Jesus.

Subject. This cry of the Greeks was that of the old Gentile world; it is that also of the Christian heart.

Point I. *The Gentile.*

That old world lying in darkness stretched forth its hands for the Truth, weary of its exploded philosophies and religious fables. It read the book of nature, but understood it not, and felt a consciousness of its inability: "How can I, except some man should guide me?" It struggled to find out some system of morality to save it from decay, but none proved satisfactory, none had a basis; it could not discover GOD's moral law, and sighed, "How can I, except some man should guide me?" It strove to pierce the black veil which hung over the future. What was there beyond death? was that annihilation, or was it a passage to something, and to what? But it discovered nothing, and sobbed, "How can I, except some man should guide me?"

That Man to guide poor Gentiledom and lead men to the three great Truths it behoved them to know, could be none other than GOD. For the three truths belonged to GOD; men must know:—

1. What GOD is.
2. What is GOD's Law.
3. What GOD has prepared beyond the grave.

GOD alone could reveal these mysteries. Man felt that he must know what was the nature of GOD, what was His law, and what was the reward for keeping, or punishment for breaking this law; for this knowledge was the key to the mystery of his life; and man under heathenism was set down with the riddle of life before him, a riddle which he could not solve, for he had not the key.

Point II. *The Christian.*

But now CHRIST has come, GOD Incarnate, and has taught mankind the truth. Now man is fully instructed as to:—

1. The nature of GOD.
2. His moral law.
3. The future prospect of man.

All that is plain and clear. Doubt is blown away, ignorance has passed as darkness from before the dawn. And yet men's hearts cry out, "We would see JESUS!" Not now because they need this knowledge, but because they have this knowledge. Now they know what the nature of GOD is, and they love GOD with a passionate longing which cannot be satisfied with aught save beholding Him. Now they know His moral law, they feel their own imperfection, and yearn for that immaculate goodness, the Ideal of Perfection which they cannot realize in their own lives. Now that they know that the future opens to them the prospect of the Beatific vision, their whole life is a cry of "Sir, we would see JESUS," to satisfy the hunger of their souls.

And, knowing the desire of men's hearts, JESUS has deigned to be present amongst the faithful, not in His unveiled glory, but hidden in mysteries. "We would see JESUS," the great heart of Christendom utters; and He answers, Behold Me! I would not leave you comfortless, I have come to you, and under the Eucharistic species behold Me! Handle Me, and see that it is I Myself. The Eucharist is the love of JESUS answering the love of man, the Divine response to the versicle, "We would see JESUS!"

Conclusion. And how may we see Him? "Blessed are the pure in heart, for they shall see GOD."

C.

THE SHAME AND GLORY OF THE CHURCH.

"*In that day shalt thou not be ashamed for all thy doings, wherein thou hast transgressed against Me: for then I will take away out of the midst of thee them that rejoice in thy pride; and thou shalt be no more haughty in* (margin) *My holy mountain.*"—Zephaniah iii. 11.

Introduction. The Church has two aspects—she is at once human and Divine. As human she is full of imperfection, evil, and error; as Divine she is perfect, holy, and infallible. That is to say, whenever she acts in her corporate capacity she is the infallible teacher of truth, whenever she is acting as the dispenser of sacraments she is holy and perfect. But whenever her members individually act independently of her, or transgress her rules, dispute her teaching, neglect her laws, then error, evil, and imperfection are the result.

Consequently, from one point of view the Church is the Bride, from another point of view she is the harlot; from one point of view she is Jerusalem, from another point she is Babylon—just as any man is good or bad according as you consider his virtues or his vices.

Point I. Now, as guilty of the sins of her members, the whole Church is bound to lament in sackcloth and ashes. And groups of individuals, composing what we call Branches of the Church, or National Churches, are just as liable to error, evil, and imperfection as are individuals, for they are only groups of members, not the entirety of the body, and it is to the whole body alone that the prerogative of infallibility is assured.

Let us take the Church of England. Three hundred years ago she broke from Catholic unity, tampered with the faith, mutilated the sacramental system, and robbed her members of privileges accorded them by CHRIST. Shame that it should be so, but for three hundred years she has boasted of her crippled, insulated condition, and has been haughty in GOD's holy mountain, glorying in her shame. And what has been the result? She has lost the ignorant, who have deserted her in tens of thousands for heresy; she has alienated the educated. "She obeyed not the voice, she received not correction, she trusted not in the LORD, she drew not near to her GOD" (Zeph. iii. 2); but put her confidence in kings and princes, and enthroned a fallible man, an adulterous king, in the place of CHRIST, as supreme Head of the Church.

"Her princes within her are roaring lions; her judges are evening wolves; they gnaw not the bones till the morrow.:" her substance has been seized by the rapacity of kings and nobles, and they fatten on her spoils; they have robbed her of her rights of self-government, of her right of nominating her chief pastors, of correcting and removing abuses.

"Her prophets are light and treacherous persons"—only think what some of the English bishops have been. Denying the Truth, fighting against GOD the HOLY GHOST; forbidding to give honour to JESUS CHRIST; in league with the World Power to persecute those who hold the faith. "Her priests have polluted the sanctuary"—oh! to think of the sacrileges that have been committed at our altars, how the Sacred Body of CHRIST has been handled and strewn about the floor; how the Catholic faith has been denied, and Catholic worship has been put aside, and the Word of GOD has been made of none effect by Protestant traditions.

Now what comes? Humiliation first. As a Church we must fall down and acknowledge our transgression, we must be ashamed for that which has been our boast, we must acknowledge that we have gone astray like sheep that are lost, deserting GOD's truth for the doctrines of men!

Point II. And then, when we have humbled ourselves, then says GOD, "I will turn to the people a pure language, that they may all call upon the name of the LORD, to serve Him with one consent." Then will come reunion, and all will be once more of one heart and mind. "From beyond the rivers of Ethiopia My suppliants, even the daughter of My dispersed, shall bring Mine offering." The dispersed, those who have been scattered through the sects by Protestantism, but yet in their darkness beyond the river, have been suppliants, they shall return, and bring the offering of true Catholic worship.

"The remnant of Israel shall not do iniquity, nor speak lies; neither shall a deceitful tongue be found in their mouth; for they shall feed and lie down," feed on the Eucharist, and lie down reposing from their wanderings in the infallibility of the Church, "and none shall make them afraid." And the promise is even fuller: of course it applies to the whole Church, but the whole Church is made up of portions. It is not the Anglican Church only which has erred and sinned; the Roman Church has much, very much for which she must humble herself, ere the sterility which has fallen on her, as it has on the English Church, shall pass away.

It is not for those who have glass windows to cast stones; but it is impossible for us to close our eyes to the terrible picture of the Papacy in the Middle Ages. By its pride it rent the robe of CHRIST, and separated the East from the

West. By its exactions, and tolerance of falsehood and evil, it made itself responsible for the fearful outbreak of the sixteenth century, and for the alienation of the Protestant world from the life-giving Sacraments, and the faith in its integrity.

We English Churchmen know what we want. We will be Catholics, but we won't be Papists. We lament what is evil amongst us, but we look to Rome also to cry "Peccavi!"

Till the Church of Rome and the Church of England have learned to humble themselves, and smite their breasts, and cry to GOD for pardon—Rome for the rapacity and pride of the Papacy, Rome for the blood she has shed with unsparing hand, Rome for her light mingling of idle fables with Divine truth; England for her mutilation of the truth, her tampering with Sacraments, her worship of the World Power, the Apocalyptic Beast—so long barrenness is theirs. But when they turn and confess, then the LORD will bless them with fruitfulness once more.

Conclusion. "Sing, O daughter of Zion; shout, O Israel; be glad and rejoice with all thy heart, O daughter of Jerusalem. The LORD hath taken away thy judgments, He hath cast out thine enemy; the King of Israel, even the LORD, is in the midst of thee: thou shalt not see evil any more. In that day it shall be said to Jerusalem, Fear thou not; and to Zion, Let not thine hands be slack . . . . . At that time I will bring you again, even in the time that I gather you; for I will make you a name and a praise among all people of the earth, when I turn back your captivity before your eyes, saith the LORD."

J. MASTERS AND CO., PRINTERS, ALBION BUILDINGS, BARTHOLOMEW CLOSE, E.C.

November, 1884.

NEW BOOKS, AND NEW EDITIONS,

PUBLISHED BY

J. MASTERS & Co., 78, NEW BOND ST., LONDON.

HARRIET MONSELL. A Memoir. By the Rev. T. T. Carter, M.A., Hon. Canon of Ch. Ch. Oxford, and Warden of the House of Mercy, Clewer. Second Edition. Imperial 16mo., cloth, with Portrait, engraved on steel by Stodart. 5s.

THE POLITY OF THE CHRISTIAN CHURCH OF EARLY, MEDIÆVAL AND MODERN TIMES. By ALEXIUS AURELIUS PELLICCIA. Translated from the original Latin by the Rev. J. C. BELLETT, M.A. 8vo., cloth, 15s.

GOD'S WITNESS IN PROPHECY AND HISTORY. Bible Studies on the Historical Fulfilments of the Prophetic Blessings on the Twelve Tribes contained in Gen. xlix, with a Supplementary Inquiry into the History of the Lost Tribes. By the Rev. J. C. BELLETT, M.A. Crown 8vo., cloth, ~~4s. 6d.~~ 6/-

OUTLINES OF CHURCH TEACHING. A Series of Instructions for the Sundays and Chief Holy Days of the Christian Year. By C. C. G. With Preface by the Rev. FRANCIS PAGET, M.A., Vicar of Bromsgrove, Examining Chaplain to the Lord Bishop of Ely, and sometime Tutor of Christ Church, Oxford. Crown 8vo., cloth, 4s. 6d.

SWEET SONGS FOR MOURNING MOTHERS. Collected and arranged by LUIGI, author of "Nanta," "Legends of the Rhine for Children," &c. Small 8vo., cloth, 3s.

CONSIDERATIONS ON THE SPIRITUAL LIFE. Suggested by Passages in the Collects for the Sundays in Lent. By the Rev. G. S. HOLLINGS, Sub-Warden of the House of Mercy, Bovey Tracey, author of "Meditations on the Divine Life," &c. Crown 8vo., cloth, 2s. 6d.

MEDITATIONS ON THE DIVINE LIFE AND THE BLESSED SACRAMENT, together with Considerations on the Transfiguration. By the Rev. G. S. HOLLINGS, author of "Helps to Meditation for Beginners." Crown 8vo., cloth, 3s. 6d.

CONSIDERATIONS ON THE WISDOM OF GOD. By the Rev. G. S. HOLLINGS, Sub-Warden of the Devon House of Mercy. Crown 8vo., cloth, 4s.

THE EVENING OF LIFE; or, Meditations and Devotions for the Aged. By the Rev. W. E. HEYGATE, M.A., Rector of Brighstone, Isle of Wight. Third Edition. Crown 8vo., cloth, 4s.

CHRISTUS CONSOLATOR. Short Meditations for Invalids, from the Writings of Dr. PUSEY, selected by a Lady. With a Preface by GEORGE E. JELF, M.A., Canon of Rochester. 2s.; roan, 3s.

GENESIS AND MODERN SCIENCE. By the Author of "Christ in the Law," &c. An Explanation of the First Chapter of the Bible in accordance with observed facts. Fcap. 8vo., 1s. 6d.

"A most useful little work, well suited for these times. It is very suitable reading for any whose faith in revelation is in danger of being undermined by the plausible assertions of modern unbelief."—*National Church*.

HELPS TO MEDITATION. Sketches for Every Day in the Year. By the Rev. A. G. MORTIMER, Rector of S. Mary's, Castleton, New York. With Introduction by the Bishop of Springfield. Vol. I. Advent to Trinity, 220 Meditations. 8vo., cloth, 7s. 6d. Third Edition. Vol. II. Trinity. Second Edition. 7s. 6d.

*** The object of this work is to supply Material for Meditation and Outlines of Sermons.

HELPS TO MEDITATION FOR BEGINNERS. By a Priest of the Church of England. Edited by the Rev. CANON BODY. 16mo., 3d.

SUGGESTIONS ON THE METHOD OF MEDITATION. By the Rev. W. B. TREVELYAN. With a Preface by the LORD BISHOP OF ELY. 2d.

ON THE NATURE AND CONSTITUTION OF THE PRESENT KINGDOM OF HEAVEN UPON EARTH. By the Rev. J. R. WEST, M.A., Vicar of Wrawby. Fcap. 8vo., cloth, 2s. 6d.

CURIOSITIES OF SUPERSTITION AND SKETCHES OF SOME UNREVEALED RELIGIONS. By W. H. DAVENPORT ADAMS, author of "Heroes of the Cross," &c. Crown 8vo., cloth, 5s.

HEROES OF THE CROSS. A Series of Biographical Studies of Saints, Martyrs, and Christian Pioneers. By W. H. DAVENPORT ADAMS. Crown 8vo., 488 pp., cloth, 7s. 6d.

"This is a handsome volume containing biographical sketches of men and women notable for their heroic conduct in the struggle to uphold the standard of the religion of CHRIST. Mr. Adams presents a fair and impartial picture of the heroes selected for delineation. A catholic tone pervades the whole book, and Mr. Adams has provided his readers with a valuable and worthy series of studies from the lives of great men and women."—*Church Times.*

THE PSALM OF THE SAINTS: a Gloss upon Psalm CXIX. Extracted from NEALE and LITTLEDALE'S Commentary on the Psalms. Crown 8vo., cloth, 3s. 6d.

SHORT DEVOTIONS FOR THE ALTAR. In large type. 18mo., cloth boards, 1s. 6d.

SPRING BUDS: COUNSELS FOR THE YOUNG. From the French. By the Translator of "Gold Dust." With a Preface by CHARLOTTE M. YONGE. 18mo., cloth, 2s.; limp cloth, 1s. 6d.; roan, 3s. 6d.; calf or morocco, 6s.

GOLD DUST SERIES.

GOLD DUST: a Collection of Golden Counsels for the Sanctification of Daily Life. Translated from the French. With Preface by CHARLOTTE M. YONGE. In Two Parts. Price of each Part, cloth gilt, 1s.; wrapper, 6d.; roan, 1s. 6d.; limp calf, 2s. 6d.

*** Parts I. and II. in one Volume, limp roan, 2s. 6d.; limp calf, 3s. 6d.

GOLD DUST. (In larger type.) Translated from the French. Edited by C. M. YONGE. Complete in 1 Vol., Imp. 2mo., cloth, full gilt sides, 2s. 6d.; roan, 3s. 6d.; calf or morocco, 6s.

GOLDEN TREASURES. Counsels for the Happiness of Daily Life. Translated and abridged from the French. Edited by the Author of "The Divine Master." Uniform with "Gold Dust," cloth gilt, 1s.; roan, 1s. 6d.; calf, 2s. 6d.

"This little book has been drawn from the same source as 'Gold Dust,' and will be found to possess all the rare qualities which won so favourable a reception for its predecessor."

SPARKS OF LIGHT FOR EVERY DAY. Collected by Madame GUIZOT DE WITT; done into English by the Translator of "Gold Dust." Edited by CHARLOTTE M. YONGE. Cloth gilt, 1s.; wrapper, 6d.; limp roan, 1s. 6d.; limp calf, 2s. 6d.

THOUGHTS ON HOLINESS, Doctrinal and Practical. By W. A. Copinger. Fcap. 8vo., cloth, 2s. 6d.

"The aim of this little book, which is full of spiritual life and light, is to set the highest privileges, responsibilities, and duties of the professing Christian in fresh lights and uncommon surroundings."—*Liverpool Mercury.*

COLLECTS, EPISTLES, AND GOSPELS, suggested for use on certain special occasions and Holy-Days. With a Preface by the Rev. T. T. Carter, M.A., Hon. Canon of Christ Church, Oxford, and Warden of the House of Mercy, Clewer. Dedicated by permission to the Lord Bishop of Oxford. Crown 8vo., 1s. 6d.

For the Use of Teachers in Church Schools.

LESSONS ON THE CHURCHYARD AND THE FABRIC OF THE CHURCH. By E. E. Jarrett. With five large sheets of illustrations on Imperial Paper by the Rev. W. Morrison, Vicar of Midsomer Norton, Bath. Price 6s.

"Full of excellent spiritual teaching derived from the ideas suggested by the architectural features and arrangements of a Church. They are excellently calculated to interest the senior class of a Sunday or Day School in their Parish Church, in ways quite new to them."—*School Guardian.*

AN ACT OF SPIRITUAL COMMUNION. By the Rev. James Skinner, M.A. With Notice by the Rev. T. T. Carter, M.A., Superior General of the Confraternity of the Blessed Sacrament. Royal 32mo., cloth, 6d.

HYMNS FOR LITTLE CHILDREN. By Mrs. C. F. Alexander. Fifty-sixth Edition, handsomely printed on thick toned paper, with red border lines, 16mo., cloth, 2s. 6d.

With Twelve Photographs, extra cloth, gilt edges, 5s.; morocco, 10s.

"This well known collection has certainly never before appeared in so attractive a form as in the beautiful little book before us. The poems need no words at this day to enhance the value they have so long possessed, but the volume in which they are now embodied is really a work of art from the exquisite photographs with which it is adorned, and the perfect taste with which the whole is arranged."—*Churchman's Companion.*

MORAL SONGS. By Mrs. C. F. Alexander. A New Illustrated Edition, with eighty-five engravings on wood from original drawings by E. M. Wimperis, R. P. Leitch, W. H. J. Boot, P. Skelton, W. Rainey, and other Artists. The illustrations have been arranged and engraved by James D. Cooper. Small 4to., cloth, 6s.

HOMEWARD BOUND. The Voyage and the Voyagers; the Pilot and the Port. By the Rev. F. E. Paget, M.A., Rector of Elford. Third edition. Crown 8vo., cloth, 4s.

"It is a review of the cares, the duties, the troubles of life; the consolations that enable souls to bear, the principles upon which it behoves them to act, the hopes that brighten the darkest prospects of the traveller through the world. It is no unworthy gift to the Church from one who has served her so well by his pen in past time."—*Literary Churchman.*

"No one can read it without being the better for it."—*Church Bells.*

A STUDENT PENITENT OF 1695. Diary, Correspondence, &c., of a Student, illustrating Academical Life at Oxford. By the Rev. F. E. Paget, M.A., Rector of Elford. Crown 8vo., cloth, 4s. 6d.

"The Diaries are very remarkable for their beauty, truth, and sound moral and spiritual perceptions. The whole book is a gem. But it is the latter part of it which charms us most. It is full of suggestiveness, and that of a very delicate and beautiful kind. For sick persons or for those who have much (or indeed anything) to do with the sick it will be most valuable."—*Literary Churchman.*

THE COPTIC MORNING SERVICE FOR THE LORD'S DAY. Translated into English by JOHN, MARQUESS OF BUTE, K.T. With the Original Coptic of those parts said aloud. Crown 8vo., cloth, 6s.

FIVE PLAIN SERMONS ON THE SACRAMENT OF THE ALTAR. By the Rev. W. H. CLEAVER, M.A. Fourth Edition. Fcap. 8vo., 1s.

SIX PLAIN SERMONS ON PENITENCE. By the Rev. W. H. CLEAVER, M.A. Fourth Edition. Fcap. 8vo., 1s.

THE LIFE OF PEACE. By the Rev. R. C. Lundin Brown, M.A., late Vicar of Rhodes, Manchester. Fcap. 8vo., cloth, 2s. 6d.

"This is a work of unusual beauty and spiritual worth. It is one that we can recommend to our readers to be put upon the shelf beside their Thomas à Kempis and 'Holy Living and Dying' for periodical use. We have had few works before us of late with which we have been so pleased."—*Literary Churchman.*

THE DEAD IN CHRIST. A Word of Consolation for Mourners. By the Rev. R. C. LUNDIN BROWN, M.A., late Vicar of Rhodes, Manchester. Third Edition, super-royal 32mo., cloth boards, 1s. 6d.; cloth limp, 1s.

ANCIENT EPITAPHS from A.D. 1250 to 1800. Collected and set forth in chronological order by T. F. RAVENSHAW, M.A., F.S.A., Rector of Pewsey, Wilts. 8vo., cloth, 7s. 6d.

A FEW PRACTICAL HINTS ON CHURCH EMBROIDERY. With six plates. 1s.

KALENDAR OF THE IMITATION: Sentences for every day of the year from the "Imitatio Christi." Translated from the edition of 1630. Edited by the late Rev. J. M. NEALE, D.D. New edition, royal 32mo., cloth, 1s.

PEARLS RE-STRUNG: Stories from the Apocrypha. By Mrs. MACKARNESS, author of "A Trap to Catch a Sunbeam," &c. 16mo., cloth, 2s. Illustrated.

"An elegant and successful treatment of some of the more marked narratives of the Apocryphal writings. Nothing could be more attractive and winning than the way in which these stories are presented here, and children will be sure to appreciate them in the new garb in which Mrs. Mackarness has clothed them."—*Literary Churchman.*

NEW ILLUSTRATED EDITION.

SACRED ALLEGORIES. By the late Rev. E. Monro, M.A. Complete in one vol. With Illustrations engraved on wood by Mr. J. D. Cooper. Crown 8vo., cloth, 7s. 6d.; morocco, 16s.

THE DARK RIVER. | THE COMBATANTS. | THE JOURNEY HOME.
THE VAST ARMY. | THE REVELLERS, &c. | THE DARK MOUNTAINS.

Cheap Editions of the Allegories separately, 1s. each, in a new and improved binding, with an illustration to each.

POCKET BOOK OF DEVOTIONS AND EXTRACTS FOR INVALIDS. By C. L. Edited by the Ven. ALFRED POTT, B.D., Archdeacon of Berkshire, Vicar of Clifton Hampden. Super royal 32mo., cloth, 1s. 6d.

CHURCH CHOIRS; containing a Brief History of the Changes in Church Music during the last Forty or Fifty Years, with Directions for the Formation, Management, and Instruction of Cathedral, Collegiate, and Parochial Choirs; being the result of thirty-six years' experience in Choir Training. By FREDERICK HELMORE. Fourth Edition, Crown 8vo., 1s.

"The hints and directions on the formation, management, and instruction of Church Choirs are simply invaluable."—*Church Times.*

SPEAKERS, SINGERS, AND STAMMERERS. With Illustrations. By FREDERICK HELMORE, author of "Church Choirs," "The Chorister's Instruction Book," &c. Crown 8vo., cloth, 4s. 6d.

"It will prove invaluable to all who are preparing to enter professions, whether music, the bar, or the pulpit."—*Public Opinion.*

"We know many manuals of elocution, and we are bound to say that this is the best we have ever seen. We perceive at once that we are in the hands of a master. There is a most valuable chapter on 'Voice Training' of which we must express a very high appreciation. This is a book which should not be left unnoticed by those who have in their charge the training of our young clergy."—*Literary Churchman.*

CHRIST IN THE LAW; or, the Gospel foreshadowed in the Pentateuch. Compiled from various sources. By a Priest of the Church of England. Third Edition. Fcap. 8vo., cloth, 3s. 6d.

"The author has apprehended, as it seems to us, the real spirit and the only true moral value of the Old Testament." —*Saturday Review.*

"A charming book and one which we should be glad to see in every hand. In the most modest form it comprises more real teaching than many an ambitious treatise."—*Literary Churchman.*

"Written with singular accuracy, moderation, and judgment."—*Church Review.*

"As a popular exegetical treatise this has had few superiors of its kind."—*Church Times.*

CHRIST IN THE PROPHETS. Joshua, Judges, Samuel, Kings. By the Author of "CHRIST in the Law." Fcap. 8vo., 4s. 6d.

"The compiler of that capital book, 'CHRIST in the Law,' has now issued a continuation under the title of 'CHRIST in the Prophets.' This volume is a worthy companion to its predecessor, and that is no small praise. We strongly advise clergymen to give both volumes of R. H. N. B.'s work to their school teachers, impressing upon them at the same time the duty of studying them carefully and of reproducing what they learn from them in the lessons they give the children."—*Church Times.*

A COMMENTARY ON THE SONG OF SONGS. By the Rev. R. F. LITTLEDALE, LL.D., D.C.L. 12mo., antique cloth, 7s.

A COMMENTARY ON THE PRAYER BOOK, for the use of Pastors and Teachers in the Church and School. By the Rev. RICHARD ADAMS, M.A., Vicar of Lever Bridge, Bolton. Fcap. 8vo., cloth, 4s.

"The younger clergy, theological students, Sunday School teachers, and in fact teachers of all grades, will find it a most serviceable manual. It gives just the matter wanted for Lessons on the Prayer Book; and for this reason any one using it will get more help from it than from any book we know."—*Literary Churchman.*

VILLAGE CONFERENCES ON THE CREED. By the Rev. S. BARING-GOULD, M.A., Vicar of Lew Trenchard, Devon; author of "Origin and Development of Religious Belief," &c. Second Edition. Crown 8vo., cloth, 3s. 6d.

"We would wish that every country parson might read and mark these sermons. The common sayings and doings, the common sights and sounds of country life, furnish their illustrations. They revert in a fuller degree and with more delicate tact than any modern sermons we know to the original type of the parables of the Gospel." —*Literary Churchman.*

ONE HUNDRED SKETCHES OF SERMONS FOR EXTEMPORE PREACHERS. By the Rev. S. BARING-GOULD, M.A., author of "Origin and Development of Religious Belief," &c. &c. Fourth Edition. Crown 8vo., cloth, 6s.

"Full of power and originality—often, too, of much beauty. Quite a book to be bought. Young men who will really study these outlines will be undergoing a process of real culture."—*Literary Churchman.*

"A really beautiful volume, which we can cordially recommend. Those who know Mr. Baring-Gould will hardly need to be told that almost every page bears upon it marks of wide research, powerful thought, and uncompromising orthodoxy. We particularly commend the frequency with which legends, stories, and other illustrations are introduced."—*Church Times.*

BY THE REV. J. M. NEALE, D.D.,

LATE WARDEN OF SACKVILLE COLLEGE, EAST GRINSTED.

Fourth Edition, Four Vols., Post 8vo., cloth, 10s. 6d. each.

A COMMENTARY ON THE PSALMS, from the Primitive and Mediæval Writers; and from the various Office-Books and Hymns of the Roman, Mozarabic, Ambrosian, Gallican, Greek, Coptic, Armenian, and Syriac Rites. By the Rev. J. M. NEALE, D.D., and the Rev. R. F. LITTLEDALE, LL.D.

⁎ A new edition of Vol. IV. is now ready, containing, besides the Index of Texts, a new INDEX OF SUBJECTS for the whole work.

The INDEX OF SUBJECTS may be had separately. Price 1s. in paper cover.

"This truly valuable and remarkable Commentary is a work which *stands almost, if not entirely, alone in the theology of England; and one to which we may fairly challenge Christendom at large to produce anything precisely corresponding.* It will be found by those who have any taste at all for such studies a rich and valuable mine to which they may again and again recur without running the slightest risk of digging out the contents too hastily."—*Guardian.*

SERMONS PREACHED IN SACKVILLE COLLEGE CHAPEL.

Second Edition. Four Vols. Crown 8vo., cloth.

Vol. I. Advent to Whitsun Day. 7s. 6d.
II. Trinity and Saints' Days. 7s. 6d.
Vol. III. Lent and Passiontide. 7s. 6d.
IV. The Minor Festivals. 6s.

"Among the several volumes of writings by the late Dr. Neale which have been recently published, we must assign the foremost place as regards general utility to the *Sermons preached in Sackville College Chapel,* which hold, as we conceive, the very highest rank amongst modern Sermons intended to instruct and comfort the unlearned and suffering, by reason of the mingled clearness and beauty, the deep teaching and the practical application with which these admirable discourses abound."—*Church Times.*

"Charming volumes."—*Literary Churchman.*

READINGS FOR THE AGED. Selected from "Sermons preached in Sackville College Chapel." By the late Rev. J. M. NEALE, D.D., Warden of the College. Crown 8vo., cloth, 6s.

"One of the most useful books probably ever issued for parochial use is the late Dr. Neale's READINGS FOR THE AGED. Being also, as it deserves to be, one of the best known books among us, it needs no recommendation at our hands."—*Literary Churchman.*

SERMONS PREACHED IN A RELIGIOUS HOUSE. Second Series. Two Vols. Fcap. 8vo., cloth, 10s.

MISERERE: the Fifty-first Psalm, with Devotional Notes. Re-printed, with additions, from "Neale's Commentary on the Psalms." Wrapper, 6d.; cloth, 1s.

"As a manual for devotional study in Advent and Lent it will be found invaluable, as those who have neither money nor leisure to expend on the vast treasury of patristical lore stored up in the Commentary aforesaid may make acquaintance with the great work through this pocket manual."—*Church Times.*

SEATONIAN PRIZE POEMS. Fcap. 8vo., 3s. 6d.

MEDIÆVAL HYMNS AND SEQUENCES, translated by the Rev. J. M. NEALE, D.D. Third Edition, with numerous additions. Royal 32mo. 2s.

HYMNS FOR CHILDREN. Three Series in One Vol. Tenth Edition. 16mo., cloth, 1s.

HYMNS FOR THE SICK. Fourth Edition. 6d.; cloth, 1s.

CHILDREN'S SERVICES.

A PLEA FOR CHILDREN'S SERVICES. By the Rev. Theodore JOHNSON, Curate of Warkton, Northamptonshire. 2d.

SIX METRICAL LITANIES FOR CHILDREN. By the same Author. 1d.; or 7s. per 100.

LITANY FOR CHILDREN, with Music. ½d., or 2s. 6d. per 100.

THE ORDER FOR A CHILDREN'S SERVICE. With Music. Compiled by HENRY DITTON-NEWMAN, Organist of S. John's, Torquay. With Pointing for both Gregorian and Anglican usage. 3rd edition. 2d., or 14s. per 100; cloth, 4d.

Published with the approval of the Archbishops of Canterbury and Dublin, and authorised for use in the Dioceses of Durham, Winchester, Ely, Peterborough, Lincoln, Bath and Wells, and Oxford.

BIBLE TRUTHS IN SIMPLE WORDS. Short Addresses to Children. By the Rev. J. E. VERNON, M.A., Vicar of Bicknoller, Somerset. Fcap. 8vo., 3s.

"As sermons the addresses are excellent, and there are very few so well suited to children as these."—*Literary Churchman.*

"We quite think that sermons such as these would be listened to by children with understanding and profit."—*Church Bells.*

Second Edition, with Two new Stories. 16mo., cloth, 2s.

SERMON STORIES FOR CHILDREN'S SERVICES AND HOME READING. By the Rev. H. HOUSMAN, author of "Readings on the Psalms."

"Having read the Easter Day Sermon story to a large congregation of children, we can speak from experience of the interest excited by this touching allegory, which appears to be the gem of the book."—*Church Bells.*

"Will be found very helpful in children's services, readings at school, and even in some of those Cottage Lectures which require to have some life and interest in them."—*The Guardian.*

SUNDAY AFTERNOONS AT AN ORPHANAGE. Sermonettes for Children. By the late Rev. J. M. NEALE, D.D. Third Edition. 18mo., cloth, 2s.

BY THE RIGHT REV. J. R. WOODFORD, D.D.,

LORD BISHOP OF ELY.

ORDINATION SERMONS preached in the Dioceses of Oxford and Winchester, 1860—72. 8vo., 6s. 6d.

"Sermons all of them striking, all of them models of careful conscientious thought and composition, and many of them very forcible and original. It is a valuable volume."—*Literary Churchman.*

"A noble volume of Sermons which are such as very few living preachers could equal."—*Church Review.*

"Pre-eminently good Sermons, well-reasoned, well wrought, happy in illustration, rich in reflection, eloquent in expression." —*Scottish Guardian.*

SERMONS PREACHED IN VARIOUS CHURCHES OF BRISTOL. Second Edition. 8vo., 7s. 6d.

OCCASIONAL SERMONS. Two Vols. Second Edition. 8vo. 7s. 6d. each.

BY THE REV. T. T. CARTER, M.A.,

LATE RECTOR OF CLEWER, HON. CANON OF CHRIST CHURCH, OXFORD, AND WARDEN OF THE HOUSE OF MERCY, CLEWER.

PARISH TEACHINGS. The Apostles' Creed and Sacraments. Crown 8vo., cloth, 4s. 6d.

SERMONS. Third Edition. 8vo., 9s.

SPIRITUAL INSTRUCTIONS. Crown 8vo., cloth.

1. THE HOLY EUCHARIST. Fifth Edition. 3s. 6d.
2. THE DIVINE DISPENSATIONS. Second Edition. 3s. 6d.
3. THE RELIGIOUS LIFE. 3s. 6d.
4. THE LIFE OF GRACE. 3s. 6d.

LENT LECTURES. Four Series in 1 Vol. Crown 8vo., cloth, 6s.

THE IMITATION OF OUR LORD. Fifth Edition. 2s. 6d. Demy 8vo.

PARISH SERMONS ON CHURCH QUESTIONS. Fcap. 8vo., 1s.

THE DOCTRINE OF THE PRIESTHOOD IN THE CHURCH OF ENGLAND. Third Edition. 4s.

THE DOCTRINE OF CONFESSION IN THE CHURCH OF ENGLAND. Second Edition. Post 8vo., 6s.

THE DOCTRINE OF THE HOLY EUCHARIST, drawn from the Holy Scriptures and the Records of the Church of England. Third Edition. Fcap. 8vo., 9d.

VOWS AND THE RELIGIOUS STATE. Crown 8vo., 2s.

FAMILY PRAYERS. Fifth Edition. 18mo., cloth, 1s.

EDITED BY THE REV. T. T. CARTER.

A BOOK OF PRIVATE PRAYER, FOR MORNING, MID-DAY, NIGHT, AND OTHER TIMES, with Rules for those who would live to GOD amid the business of daily life. Eleventh Edition. Limp cloth, 1s.; cl., red edges, 1s. 3d.; roan, 1s. 6d.; French morocco, 2s.; limp calf, 3s. 6d.

LITANIES, and other Devotions. Second Edition. 1s. 6d.

MEMORIALS FOR USE IN A RELIGIOUS HOUSE. Second Edition Enlarged. 6d.

NIGHT OFFICE FOR CHRISTMAS. 6d.

THE FOOTPRINTS OF THE LORD ON THE KING'S HIGH-WAY OF THE CROSS. Devotional Aids for Holy Week. Fcap. 8vo., cloth, 1s.

FOOTSTEPS OF THE HOLY CHILD, being Readings on the Incarnation. Part I., 1s. Part II., 2s. 6d. In One Vol., 3s. 6d. cloth.

MANUAL OF DEVOTION FOR SISTERS OF MERCY. In Eight Parts, or Two Vols., cloth, 10s.

SIMPLE LESSONS; or, Words Easy to be Understood. A Manual of Teaching. Three Parts in one Volume. Third Edition. 18mo., cloth, 3s.

BY THE REV. W. H. HUTCHINGS, M.A.

Second Edition revised. Crown 8vo., cloth, 4s.

THE LIFE OF PRAYER. A Course of Lectures.

"Nothing can be more delightful than the way in which the author of these Lectures has treated a devotional subject of the very first rank and absolutely needful for every Christian."—*Church Quarterly.*

"It is eminently wise and pious. We do not know any work at once so full and so concise, so sympathetic and so systematic."—*Literary Churchman.*

Third Edition, revised and enlarged. With an Index, crown 8vo., cloth, 4s. 6d.

THE PERSON AND WORK OF THE HOLY GHOST. A Doctrinal and Devotional Treatise.

"Readers of Mr. Hutchings' valuable work will welcome this new and improved edition. From a Course of Lectures it has become a Treatise. We may hope that it will become of permanent use to the Church."—*Church Quarterly.*

Second Edition, crown 8vo., cloth, 4s.

SOME ASPECTS OF THE CROSS.

"A thorough and profound treatise on this subject written with great power of analysis and with a noteworthy combination of soberness and depth."—*Guardian.*

BOOKS FOR THE USE OF THE CLERGY.

Sixth Edition, much enlarged.

THE PRIEST'S PRAYER BOOK, with a brief Pontifical. Containing Private Prayers and Intercessions; Offices, Readings, Prayers, Litanies, and Hymns, for the Visitation of the Sick; Offices for Bible and Confirmation Classes, Cottage Lectures, &c.; Notes on Confession, Direction, Missions, and Retreats; Remedies for Sin; Anglican Orders; Bibliotheca Sacerdotalis, &c., &c.

One Vol. cloth . . . 6s. 6d. Two Vols. cloth . . . 7s. 6d.
One Vol. calf or morocco 10s. 6d.

Reprinted from "The Priest's Prayer Book,"

RESPONSAL TO THE OFFICES OF THE SICK. For the Use of Attendants. Cloth, 1s.
PAROCHIAL OFFICES. 1d. SCHOOL OFFICES. 1d.
OFFICE FOR A RURIDECANAL SYNOD OR CLERICAL MEETING. 1d.
ANGLICAN ORDERS. A Summary of Historical Evidence. 1d.
OFFICE FOR THE ADMISSION OF A CHORISTER. 1d.

EMBER HOURS. By the Rev. W. E. HEYGATE, M.A., Rector of Brighstone, Isle of Wight. Third Edition Revised, with an Essay on RELIGION IN RELATION TO SCIENCE, by the Rev. T. S. ACKLAND, M.A., Vicar of Newton Wold, author of "Story of Creation," &c. Fcap. 8vo., cloth, 3s.

MEMORIALE VITÆ SACERDOTALIS; or, Solemn Warnings of the Great Shepherd, JESUS CHRIST, to the Clergy of His Holy Church. From the Latin of Arvisenet. Adapted to the Use of the Anglican Church by the late BISHOP OF BRECHIN. Third edition, Fcap. 8vo., cloth, 3s. 6d.; calf, 6s.

MEMORANDA PAROCHIALIA, or the Parish Priest's Pocket Book. By the Rev. F. E. PAGET, M.A., Rector of Elford. 3s. 6d., double size 5s.

THE BOOK OF COMMON PRAYER OF 1662, according to the *Sealed Copy* in the Tower. Printed in red and black, fcap. 8vo., cloth, 2s. 6d.

THE CHURCHMAN'S DIARY: an Almanack and Directory for the Celebration of the Service of the Church. 4d.; interleaved, 6d.; cloth, 10d.; roan tuck, 2s.

SERMONS REGISTER, for Ten Years, by which an account may be kept of Sermons, the number, subject, and when preached. Post 4to., 1s.

REGISTER OF SERMONS, PREACHERS, NUMBER OF COMMUNICANTS, AND AMOUNT OF OFFERTORY. Fcap. 4to., bound, 4s. 6d. (The Book of Strange Preachers as ordered by the 52nd Canon.)

REGISTER OF PERSONS CONFIRMED AND ADMITTED TO HOLY COMMUNION. For 500 names, 4s. 6d. For 1000 names, 7s. 6d. half-bound.

THE LITANY, TOGETHER WITH THE LATTER PART OF THE COMMINATION SERVICE NOTED. Edited by RICHARD REDHEAD. Handsomely printed in red and black. Demy 4to., wrapper, 7s. 6d.; imitation morocco, 18s.; best morocco, 24s.; morocco panelled, &c., 30s.

THE LITTLE HOURS OF THE DAY, according to the Kalendar of the Church of England. Complete Edition, crown 8vo., cloth, 3s. 6d.; wrapper, 2s. 6d.

HORARIUM; seu Libellus Precationum, Latinè editus. 18mo., cl. 1s.

THE CLERGYMAN'S MANUAL OF PRIVATE PRAYERS. Collected and Compiled from Various Sources. A Companion Book to "The Priest's Prayer Book." Cloth, 1s.

THE PRIEST IN HIS INNER LIFE. Fcap. 8vo., cloth, 1s.

DEVOTIONAL BOOKS.

BENEATH THE CROSS. Readings for Children on our LORD'S Seven Sayings. By FLORENCE WILFORD. Edited by CHARLOTTE M. YONGE. 18mo., cloth boards, 1s. 6d.; limp cloth, 1s.

THE LOVE OF THE ATONEMENT, a Devotional Exposition of the Fifty-third chapter of Isaiah. By the Right Rev. R. MILMAN, D.D., Bishop of Calcutta. Fifth Edition. Fcap. 8vo., cloth, 3s. 6d.; calf, 8s.

MEDITATIONS ON THE SUFFERING LIFE OF OUR LORD. Translated from Pinart. Adapted to the use of the Anglican Church by A. P. FORBES, D.C.L., Bishop of Brechin. Fifth Edition. Fcap. 8vo., cloth, 5s.; calf, 10s.

NOURISHMENT OF THE CHRISTIAN SOUL. Translated from Pinart. Adapted to the use of the Anglican Church by A. P. FORBES, D.C.L., Bishop of Brechin. Fourth Edition. Fcap. 8vo., cloth, 5s.; calf, 10s.

THE MIRROR OF YOUNG CHRISTIANS. Translated from the French. Edited by A. P. FORBES, D.C.L., Bishop of Brechin. With Engravings, 2s. 6d.; morocco antique, 7s.

THE DIVINE MASTER: a Devotional Manual illustrating the Way of the Cross. With Ten steel Engravings. Ninth Edition. 2s. 6d.; morocco, 5s. Cheap Edition, in wrapper, 1s.

THE SHADOW OF THE HOLY WEEK. By the Author of "The Divine Master." 18mo., cloth, 1s.

THE PSALTER, or Seven Ordinary Hours of Prayer, according to the Use of the Church of Sarum. Beautifully printed and illustrated. Fcap. 4to., antique binding. Reduced to 15s.

THE DIVINE LITURGY: a Manual of Devotions for the Sacrament of the Altar. For those who communicate. FOURTH EDITION, revised, with additional Prayers and Hymns, limp cloth, 1s. 6d. A superior edition printed on toned paper, cloth boards, red edges, 2s. 6d.

A FEW DEVOTIONAL HELPS FOR THE CHRISTIAN SEASONS. Edited by Two Clergymen. Two Vols., cloth, 5s. 6d.

COMMUNION WITH GOD. Meditations and Prayers for One Week. By a Clergyman. Fcap. 8vo., cloth, 2s.

THE KALENDAR OF THE IMITATION: Sentences for every day of the year from the "Imitatio Christi." Translated from the edition of 1630. Edited by the Rev. J. M. NEALE, D.D. New edition, royal 32mo., cloth, 1s.

THE GREAT TRUTHS OF THE CHRISTIAN RELIGION. Edited by the Rev. W. U. RICHARDS, M.A. Sixth Edition. Fcap. 8vo. cloth, 3s.; calf, 8s.

MEDITATIONS ON THE MOST PRECIOUS BLOOD AND EXAMPLE OF CHRIST. By the Rev. J. S. TUTE, M.A., Vicar of Markington, Yorkshire. Fcap. 8vo., cloth, 1s.

SPIRITUAL VOICES FROM THE MIDDLE AGES. Consisting of a Selection of Abstracts from the Writings of the Fathers, adapted for the Hour of Meditation, and concluding with a Biographical Notice of their Lives. 3s. 6d.

PRAYERS AND MAXIMS. In large type. Fourth Edition. Crown 8vo. cloth, 2s. 6d.

THE SOLILOQUY OF THE SOUL, and THE GARDEN OF ROSES. Translated from Thomas à Kempis. By the Rev. W. B. FLOWER, B.A. 2s.

THE HOUR OF DEATH. A Manual of Prayers and Meditations intended chiefly for those who are in Sorrow or in Sickness. By the Rev. J. B. WILKINSON. Royal 32mo., 2s.

MEDITATIONS ON OUR LORD'S PASSION. Translated from the Armenian of Matthew, Vartabed. 2s. 6d.

SELECTIONS, NEW AND OLD. With a Preface by Bishop WILBERFORCE. Fcap. 8vo., 4s. 6d.

THE HIDDEN LIFE. Translated from Nepveu's Pensées Chrétiennes. Fourth Edition, enlarged. 18mo., 2s.

TWELVE SHORT AND SIMPLE MEDITATIONS ON THE SUFFERINGS OF OUR LORD JESUS CHRIST. Edited by the Rev. CANON BUTLER. 2s. 6d.

THE FOOTPRINTS OF THE LORD ON THE KING'S HIGHWAY OF THE CROSS. Devotional Aids for Holy Week. Edited by the Rev. T. T. CARTER. Fcap. 8vo., cloth, 1s.

FOOTSTEPS OF THE HOLY CHILD, being Readings on the Incarnation. Edited by the Rev. T. T. CARTER. Part I., fcap. 8vo., 1s. Part II., 2s. 6d. In One Vol. cloth, 3s. 6d.

COMPANION FOR LENT. Being an Exhortation to Repentance, from the Syriac of S. Ephraem; and Thoughts for Every Day in Lent, gathered from other Eastern Fathers and Divines. By the Rev. S. C. MALAN, M.A. 1s. 3d.

THE CHRISTIAN'S DAY. By the Rev. F. E. PAGET, M.A. Royal 32mo., 2s. cloth; 5s. morocco.

MEDITATIONS FOR EVERY WEEK IN THE CHRISTIAN YEAR. By the Compiler of "Plain Prayers," with an Introduction by the Rev. CANON BUTLER, M.A., Vicar of Wantage. Second Edition. 18mo., cloth, 1s. 6d.

THE SEVEN WORDS FROM THE CROSS. A Devotional Commentary. By BELLARMINE. Second Edition. 1s. 6d.

THE THREE HOURS AGONY: Meditations, Prayers, and Hymns on the Seven Words from the Cross of our Most Holy Redeemer, together with Additional Devotions on the Passion. 4d.

EUCHARISTIC MEDITATIONS FOR A MONTH ON THE MOST HOLY COMMUNION. Translated from the French of Avrillon. Limp cloth, 2s. 6d.

DAILY MEDITATIONS: from Ancient Sources. Advent. Cloth, 1s.

DAILY MEDITATIONS FOR A MONTH, on some of the more Moving Truths of Christianity; in order to determine the Soul to be in earnest in the love and Service of her GOD. From Ancient Sources. Cloth, 1s.

A TREATISE OF THE VIRTUE OF HUMILITY, abridged from the Spanish of Rodriguez; for the use of persons living in the world. Cloth, 1s.

CONSIDERATIONS ON MYSTERIES OF THE FAITH, newly Translated and Abridged from the Original Spanish of Luis de Granada. 2s. cloth.

SPIRITUAL EXERCISES: Readings for a Retreat of Seven Days. Translated and Abridged from the French of Bourdaloue. 1s. 6d.

AIDS TO CATECHISING.

CATECHISINGS ON THE PRAYER BOOK. By the Ven. W. LEA, M.A., Archdeacon of Worcester. Third Edition. 18mo., cloth, 1s.

A CATECHISM ON THE BOOK OF COMMON PRAYER. By the Rev. ALEXANDER WATSON. 18mo., cloth, 2s.

A CATECHISM OF THEOLOGY. Second Edition, revised. 18mo., cloth, 1s. 6d.; wrapper, 1s.

THE CHURCH CATECHISM DEVELOPED. By WALTER HILMAY PIERSEY. 18mo., 4d.

A CATECHISM ON THE CHURCH. By the Rev. J. R. WEST, M.A., Vicar of Wrawby. New Edition. 4d.

CATECHISM OF THE CHIEF THINGS WHICH A CHRISTIAN OUGHT TO KNOW AND BELIEVE TO HIS SOUL'S HEALTH. Edited by several Clergymen. New Edition. 2d.

THE EVENING MEETINGS; or, the Pastor among the Boys of his Flock. By C. M. S. Fcap. 8vo., 2s.

By the Author of "The Churchman's Guide to Faith and Piety."

DEVOTIONS FOR THE SICK ROOM, PRAYERS IN SICKNESS, &c. Cloth, 2s. 6d.

COMPANION FOR THE SICK ROOM: being a Compendium of Christian Doctrine. 2s. 6d.

OFFICES FOR THE SICK AND DYING. Reprinted from the above. 1s.

LEAFLETS FOR THE SICK AND DYING; supplementary to the Offices for the same in "The Churchman's Guide to Faith and Piety." First Series. Price per set of eight, 6d.; cardboard, 9d.

MANUALS OF PRAYER.

THE DAY HOURS OF THE CHURCH OF ENGLAND, newly Translated and Arranged according to the Prayer Book and the Authorised Translation of the Bible. Fifteenth Thousand. Crown 8vo., wrapper, 1s.; cloth, 1s. 6d.

An Edition on large toned paper. Wrapper, 2s.; cloth, 2s. 6d.

THE ORDER FOR PRIME, TERCE, SEXT, NONE, AND COMPLINE, ACCORDING TO THE USE OF THE CHURCH OF ENGLAND. Newly revised. 9d. in wrapper.

This is printed in a form suitable for binding with the various editions of the Prayer Book from 24mo. to crown 8vo.

THE SERVICE FOR CERTAIN HOLYDAYS. Being a Supplement to "The Day Hours of the Church of England." Crown 8vo., 2s.

THE DAY OFFICE OF THE CHURCH, according to the Kalendar of the Church of England; consisting of Lauds, Vespers, Prime, Terce, Sext, None, and Compline, throughout the Year. To which are added, the Order for the Administration of the Reserved Eucharist, Penance, and Unction; together with the Office of the Dead, Commendation of a Soul, divers Benedictions and Offices, and full Rubrical Directions.

A complete Edition, especially for Sisterhoods and Religious Houses. By the Editor of "The Little Hours of the Day." Crown 8vo., 4s. 6d.; cloth, red edges, 5s. 6d.

THE CHURCHMAN'S GUIDE TO FAITH AND PIETY. A Manual of Instruction and Devotions. Compiled by ROBERT BRETT. Fifth Edition. Cloth, 3s. 6d.; antique calf or plain morocco, 8s. 6d. Two Vols., cloth, 4s.; limp calf, 11s.; limp morocco, 12s.

THE PRIMER, set forth at large with many Godly and Devout Prayers. Edited, from the Post-Reformation Recension, by the Rev. GERARD MOULTRIE, M.A., Vicar of South Leigh. Fourth Thousand. 18mo., cloth, 3s.

THE HOURS OF THE PRIMER. Published separately for the use of individual members of a household in Family Prayer. 18mo., cloth, 1s.

MANUAL OF DEVOTION FOR SISTERS OF MERCY. Edited by the Rev. T. T. CARTER, M.A. In Eight Parts or Two Vols. cloth, 10s.

A BOOK OF PRIVATE PRAYER FOR MORNING, MID-DAY, NIGHT, AND OTHER TIMES, with Rules for those who would live to GOD amid the business of Daily Life. Edited by the Rev. T. T. CARTER. Eleventh Edition. Limp cloth, 1s.; cloth, red edges, 1s. 3d.; roan, 1s. 6d.; French morocco, 2s.; limp calf, 3s. 6d.

THE MANUAL: a Book of Devotion. By the Rev. W. E. HEYGATE. Twenty-first Edition. Cloth limp, 1s.; boards, 1s. 3d.; leather, 1s. 6d.; French morocco, 2s.; limp calf, 3s. 6d. Cheap Edition, 6d. A Superior Edition, 12mo., cloth, 1s. 6d.

SURSUM CORDA: Aids to Private Devotion. Collected from the Writings of English Churchmen. Compiled by the Rev. F. E. PAGET. 2s. 6d. cloth.

THE MANTLE OF PRAYER; a Book of Devotions, compiled chiefly from those of Bishop Andrewes. By A. N. With a Preface by the Rev. W. J. BUTLER, M.A., Canon of Worcester. Fcap. 8vo., cloth, 1s. 6d.; roan, 2s. 6d.

CHRISTIAN SERVANT'S BOOK of Devotion, Self-Examination, and Advice. Sixth Edition. Cloth, 1s.

POCKET MANUAL OF PRAYERS FOR THE HOURS, &c., with the Collects from the Prayer Book. New Edition. Royal 32mo., cloth, 1s.; limp roan, 2s.; calf, 3s.

This popular Manual has been revised by several clergymen, and important additions have been made for the purpose of rendering it more suitable for private use, and especially for Retreats.

THE POCKET BOOK OF DAILY PRAYERS. Translated from Eastern Originals. By the Rev. S. C. MALAN, M.A. Suited for the Waistcoat Pocket. Cloth, 6d.; roan, 1s.

DEVOTIONS FOR DAILY USE. With Preface by the Hon. and Rev. Canon COURTENAY. Royal 32mo., cloth extra, 1s.

A MANUAL OF PRIVATE DEVOTIONS, containing Prayers for each Day in the Week, Devotions for the Holy Communion, and for the Sick. By BISHOP ANDREWES. 6d.; cloth, 9d.

A COLLECTION OF PRIVATE DEVOTIONS FOR THE HOURS OF PRAYER. By BISHOP COSIN. 1s.

THE CHRISTIAN'S PLAIN GUIDE. By the Rev. WALTER A. GRAY, M.A., Vicar of Arksey. 32mo., cloth boards, 1s. Cheap Edition, wrapper, 6d.

THE DEVOUT CHORISTER. Thoughts on his Vocation, and a Manual of Devotions for his use. By THOMAS F. SMITH, B.D. 32mo., cloth, 1s.

A MANUAL OF DEVOTIONS FOR SCHOOL-BOYS. Compiled from various sources. By R. BRETT. 6d.

PRAYERS FOR LITTLE CHILDREN AND YOUNG PERSONS. By R. BRETT. 6d.; cloth, 8d. Part I. 3d., cloth 4d.; Part II. 4d., cloth 6d.

THE YOUNG CHURCHMAN'S MANUAL. Second Edition. 6d.

FAMILY PRAYERS.

BOOK OF FAMILY PRAYERS, collected from the Public Liturgy of the Church of England. By E. G., Minor Canon of Durham. 2s.

PRAYERS FOR A CHRISTIAN HOUSEHOLD, chiefly taken from the Scriptures, from the Ancient Liturgies, and the Book of Common Prayer. By the Rev. T. BOWDLER. Fcap. 8vo., cloth, 2s. 6d.

FAMILY DEVOTIONS FOR A FORTNIGHT. Compiled from the Works of BISHOP ANDREWES, KEN, WILSON, KETTLEWELL, NELSON, SPINCKES, &c. (Suited also for private use.) New Edition. Fcap. 8vo., cloth, 1s. 6d.

PRAYERS AND LITANIES, taken from Holy Scripture, together with a Calendar and Table of Lessons. Arranged by the Rev. J. S. B. MONSELL, LL.D. 16mo., cloth, 1s.

FAMILY PRAYERS adapted to the course of the Ecclesiastical Year. By the Rev. R. A. SUCKLING. 6d.; cloth, 1s.

PRAYERS FOR FAMILY USE. From Ancient Sources. With Preface by the Archdeacon of S. Alban's. Fcap. 8vo., cloth, 1s.

VOLUMES OF SERMONS AND LECTURES.

ASHLEY, REV. J. M.—THE VICTORY OF THE SPIRIT: a Course of Short Sermons by way of Commentary on the Eighth Chapter of S. Paul's Epistle to the Romans. Fcap. 8vo., cloth, 2s.

——— THIRTEEN SERMONS FROM THE QUARESIMALE OF QUIRICO ROSSI. Translated from the Italian. Edited by J. M. ASHLEY, B.C.L. Fcap. 8vo., cloth, 3s. 6d.

BAINES, REV. J.—SERMONS. Fcap. 8vo., 5s.

BRECHIN, THE LATE BP. OF.—ARE YOU BEING CONVERTED? Sermons on Serious Subjects. Third Edition. Fcap. 8vo., 2s.

—— SERMONS ON AMENDMENT OF LIFE. Second Edition. Fcap. 8vo. 2s.

—— SERMONS ON THE GRACE OF GOD, and other Cognate Subjects. 3s. 6d.

CURRIE.—SERMONS AND LECTURES, FOR SUNDAYS AND HOLY DAYS FROM ADVENT TO TRINITY. By the Rev. JAMES CURRIE, M.A., late Rector of West Lavington. Demy 8vo., 7s. 6d.

BUTLER, REV. W. J.—SERMONS FOR WORKING MEN. Second Edition. 12mo., 6s. 6d.

CHAMBERLAIN, REV. T.—THE THEORY OF CHRISTIAN WORSHIP. Second Edition. 3s. 6d.

—— THE SEVEN AGES OF THE CHURCH as indicated in the Messages to the Seven Churches of Asia. Post 8vo., 3s.

CHANTER, REV. J. M.—SERMONS. 12mo., 3s. 6d.

CODD, REV. E. T.—SERMONS addressed to a Country Congregation, including Four preached before the University of Cambridge. Third Series. 12mo., 6s. 6d.

DAVIDSON, REV. J. P. F.—THE HOLY COMMUNION. A Course of Sermons. Second Edition. Fcap. 8vo., cloth, 1s. 6d.

EVANS, REV. A. B., D.D.—CHRISTIANITY IN ITS HOMELY ASPECTS: Sermons on Various Subjects. Second Series. 12mo., 3s.

FLOWER, REV. W. B.—SERMONS FOR THE SEASONS OF THE CHURCH, translated from S. Bernard. 8vo., 3s. 6d.

GALTON, REV. J. L.—ONE HUNDRED AND FORTY-TWO LECTURES ON THE BOOK OF REVELATION. In Two Vols. Fcap. 8vo., 18s.

—— NOTES OF LECTURES ON THE BOOK OF CANTICLES OR SONG OF SOLOMON, delivered in the Parish Church of S. Sidwell, Exeter. 6s.

GRESLEY, REV. W.—SERMONS PREACHED AT BRIGHTON. 12mo., 3s. 6d.

HAMILTON, REV. L. R.—PAROCHIAL SERMONS. Fcap. 8vo. 3s. 6d.

IRONS, REV. W. J., D.D.—THE PREACHING OF CHRIST. A Series of Sixty Sermons for the People. In a Packet, 5s.; cloth, 6s.

—— THE MIRACLES OF CHRIST: being a Second Series of Sermons for the People. Second Edition. 8vo., 6s.

LEA, THE VEN. ARCHDEACON.—SERMONS ON THE PRAYER BOOK. Fcap. 8vo., 2s.

LEE, REV. F. G., D.C.L.—MISCELLANEOUS SERMONS, by Clergymen of the Church of England. Edited by F. G. LEE. Crown 8vo., 3s. 6d.

MILLARD, REV. F. M.—S. PETER'S DENIAL OF CHRIST. Seven Short Sermons to Boys. Fcap. 8vo., 1s. 4d.

NEWLAND, REV. H.—POSTILS; Short Sermons on the Parables, &c., adapted from the Fathers. Second Edition. Fcap. 8vo., 3s.

NUGEE, REV. G.—THE WORDS FROM THE CROSS AS APPLIED TO OUR OWN DEATHBEDS. Second Edition. Fcap. 8vo., 2s. 6d.

PAGET, REV. F. E.—SERMONS ON THE SAINTS' DAYS. 12mo., 3s. 6d.

——— SERMONS FOR SPECIAL OCCASIONS. Crown 8vo., 5s.

PRICHARD, REV. J. C.—SERMONS. Fcap. 8vo., 4s. 6d.

PRYNNE, REV. G. R.—PLAIN PAROCHIAL SERMONS. Second Series. 8vo., 10s. 6d.

——— PAROCHIAL SERMONS (New Volume.) 8vo., 10s. 6d.

POTT, THE VEN. ARCHDEACON.—CONFIRMATION LECTURES delivered to a Village Congregation in the Diocese of Oxford. 3rd Edition. 2s.

SUCKLING, REV. R. A.—SERMONS PLAIN AND PRACTICAL. Fourth Edition. Fcap. 8vo., 3s. 6d.

SERMONS BY VARIOUS CONTRIBUTORS ILLUSTRATING THE OFFICES OF THE PRAYER BOOK. 8vo., 3s. 6d.

THOMPSON, REV. H.—CONCIONALIA. Outlines of Sermons for Parochial Use throughout the Year. Dedicated, by permission, to the LORD BISHOP OF BATH AND WELLS. First Series. Third Edition. Fcap. 8vo., 7s. 6d.

——— CONCIONALIA. Second Series. Fcap. 8vo., 6s. 6d.

TOMLINS, REV. R.—SERMONS for the Greater Cycle of High Days in the Church's Year, with Sermons for Special and Ordinary Occasions. Second Edition. 12mo., 5s.

——— ADVENT SERMONS. Illustrated by copious references to the Advent Services. Second Edition. First and Second Series, in One Vol., cloth, 2s. 6d.

WATSON, REV. A.—THE SEVEN SAYINGS ON THE CROSS. 8vo., 3s. 6d.

——— JESUS THE GIVER AND FULFILLER OF THE NEW LAW. Eight Sermons on the Beatitudes. 8vo., 3s. 6d.

WEST, REV. J. R.—SERMONS ON THE ASCENSION OF OUR LORD. Fcap. 8vo., 3s. 6d.

——— PARISH SERMONS FOR THE ADVENT AND CHRISTMAS SEASONS. Fcap. 8vo., 3s.

——— PARISH SERMONS ON THE HOLY EUCHARIST. Fcap. 8vo., cloth, 4s. 6d.

WILKINSON, REV. J. B.—MISSION SERMONS. Third Series. Fcap. 8vo., 6s.

WINDSOR, REV. S. B.—SERMONS FOR SOLDIERS preached at Home and Abroad. Fcap. 8vo., 3s. 6d.

WOOD, REV. S. THEODORE.—THE REVOLT OF MAN FROM GOD. An Advent Course of Four Sermons, Addresses to Men. 1s.

WROTH, REV. W. R.—FIVE SERMONS ON SOME OF THE OLD TESTAMENT TYPES OF HOLY BAPTISM. Post 8vo., 3s.

www.ingramcontent.com/pod-product-compliance
Lightning Source LLC
Chambersburg PA
CBHW020613030726
47497CB00007B/2214

* 9 7 8 3 7 4 1 1 9 4 1 5 3 *